'You're a provocative little package of dynamite, Serena Fleming.'

Nic looked at her with burning eyes as he continued, 'Can I take it you'll be staying the night? You're not going to make some excuse about having to go home to your sister and niece?'

'They're away for the night.'

'Aha! So you came here planning to seduce me.' He grinned, triumph dancing into his eyes. 'Got you!'

'Is that what it's all about to you, Nic? Winning? Am I just another notch on your bedpost?'

'Another notch?' he repeated incredulously. 'There's never been a notch like you in my entire life. You can take that as gospel!'

Initially a French/English teacher, **Emma Darcy** changed careers to computer programming before marriage, motherhood, and the happy demands of keeping up with three lively sons and the very social life of her businessman husband, Frank. Very much a people person, and always interested in relationships, she finds the world of romance fiction a thrilling one.

Emma Darcy is the award-winning Australian author of more than 80 Modern Romance® novels. Her compelling, sexy, intensely emotional novels have gripped the imagination of readers around the globe. She's sold nearly 60 million books worldwide and won enthusiastic praise:

'Emma Darcy delivers a spicy love story…a fiery conflict and a hot sensuality'.

—*Romantic Times*

THE BILLIONAIRE BRIDEGROOM

BY
EMMA DARCY

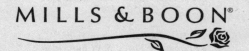
MILLS & BOON®

First published in Great Britain 2003
Harlequin Mills & Boon Limited,
Eton House, 18-24 Paradise Road, Richmond, Surrey TW9 1SR

© Emma Darcy 2003

ISBN 0 263 83229 5

Set in Times Roman 10½ on 12¼ pt.
01-0503-43474

Printed and bound in Spain
by Litografia Rosés, S.A., Barcelona

CHAPTER ONE

Wow! Definitely a million-dollar property! Real class, Serena Fleming decided appreciatively, driving the van past perfectly manicured lawns to the architect designed house owned by one of her sister's clients, Angelina Gifford. Michelle's Pet Grooming Salon drew quite a few wealthy people who used the mobile service provided, but Serena was more impressed with this place than any other she had visited in the course of picking up pampered dogs and cats.

Michelle had told her the land in this area had only been released for development four years ago. The Giffords had certainly bought a prime piece of real estate—three acres sited on top of a hill overlooking Terrigal Beach and a vast stretch of ocean. There were no formal gardens, just a few artistically placed palm trees—big fat pineapple-shaped palms with a mass of fronds growing out of the top. Must have cost a fortune to transport and plant them, all fully grown, but then quite clearly the whole place had to have cost a fortune.

The fabulous view was cut off as the van drew level with the house which seemed to have walled courtyards on this western side. All the windows would face north and east, Serena thought. Still, even the wall arrangement was interesting, painted in dark blue with a rich cream trim, suggesting sea and sand.

She brought the van to a halt adjacent to the front

door, cut the engine and hopped out, curious to meet the man who had designed all this. Nic Moretti was his name, a highly successful architect, also the brother of Angelina Gifford, whose husband had whisked her off for a trip overseas. The talented Nic had been left in charge of the house and Angelina's adored dog, Cleo, who was due for a clip and shampoo this morning.

No doubt it was convenient for him to stay here. According to the local newspaper, his design had just won the contract to build a people's park with various pavilions on crown land overlooking Brisbane Water. Easy for him to supervise the work from such a close vantage point, a mere half hour drive to the location of the proposed park.

Serena rang the doorbell and waited. And waited. She glanced at her watch. It was now ten minutes past the nine o'clock appointment. She rang the doorbell again, with considerably more vigour.

In her other life as a hair stylist in a very fashionable Sydney salon, it was always rich people who disregarded time, expecting to be fitted in whenever they arrived. Here she was on the Central Coast, a good hour and a half north of Sydney, but it was obviously no different, she thought on a disgruntled sigh. The wealthy expected others to wait on them. In fact, they expected the whole world to revolve around them.

Like her ex-fiancé…

Serena was scowling over the memory of what Lyall Duncan had expected of *her* when the door she faced was abruptly flung open.

'Yes?' a big brute of a man snapped.

Serena's jaw dropped. His thick black hair was rumpled. His unshaven jaw bristled with aggression. His muscular and very male physique was barely clothed by a pair of exotic—or was it erotic?—silk boxer shorts. And if she wasn't mistaken—*no, don't look there!* She wrenched her gaze up from the distracting bulge near his groin, took a deep breath and glared straight back at glowering dark eyes framed by ridiculously long thick eyelashes that were totally wasted on a man.

Italian heritage, of course. What else could it be with names like Nic and Angelina Moretti?

'I'm Serena from Michelle's Pet Grooming Salon,' she announced.

He frowned at her, the dark eyes sharper now as he scrutinised her face; blue eyes, pert nose, full-lipped mouth, slight cleft in her chin, wisps of blond hair escaping from the fat plait that gathered in the rest of it. His gaze dropped to the midriff top that outlined her somewhat perky breasts and the denim shorts that left her long shapely legs on full display, making Serena suddenly self-conscious of being almost as naked as he was, though definitely more decently dressed.

'Do I know you?' he barked.

He'd probably been a Doberman pinscher in another life, Serena was thinking, just before the shock of recognition kicked her heart.

'No!' she answered with panicky speed, not wanting *him* to make the link that had suddenly shot through her mind.

It had been a month ago. A whole rotten month of working fiercely at putting the still very raw experience in the irretrievable past; breaking off her engagement to Lyall, leaving her job, leaving Sydney, taking wound-licking refuge with her sister. To be suddenly faced with the *architect* of those decisions...

She could feel her forehead going clammy, the blood draining from her face as her mind screamed at the unfairness of it all. Her hands clenched, fighting the urge to lash out at him. A persistent thread of common sense argued it wasn't Nic Moretti's fault. He'd simply been the instrument who'd drawn out the true picture of her future if she went ahead with her fairy-tale marriage—Cinderella winning the Prince!

He was the man Lyall had been talking to *that night,* the man who'd expressed surprise at the high-flying property dealer, Lyall Duncan, for choosing to marry *down,* taking a lowly hairdresser as his wife. And Serena had overheard Lyall's reply—the reply that had ripped the rose-coloured spectacles off her face and shattered all her illusions. This man had heard it, too, and the humiliation of it forced her into a defensive pretence.

'Since I don't know you...' she half lied in desperate defence.

'Nic Moretti,' he rumbled at her.

'...I don't see how you can know me,' she concluded emphatically.

He'd seen her at Lyall's party but they hadn't been introduced, and she'd been all glammed up for the occasion, not in her *au naturel* state as she was this morning. Surely he wouldn't make the connection. The environment was completely different. Yet despite her denial of any previous encounter with him, he was still frowning, trying to place her.

'I'm here to collect Cleo,' she stated briskly, hating this nasty coincidence and wanting to get away as fast as possible.

'Cleo,' he repeated in a disconnected fashion.

'The dog,' she grated out.

The expression on his rugged handsome face underwent a quick and violent change, the brooding search for her identity clicking straight into totally fed up frustration. 'You mean the monster,' he flashed at her derisively.

The blood that had drained from her face, surged to her head again, making Serena see red. It was impossible to resist giving this snobby man a dose of the condescension he ladled out himself.

'I would hardly characterise a sweet little Australian silky terrier as a monster,' she said loftily.

'Sweet!' He thrust out a brawny forearm marked with long and rather deep scratches. 'Look what she did to me!'

'Mmm…' Serena felt no sympathy, silently applauding the terrier for doing the clawing this man very likely deserved. 'Raises the question…what did you do to her?'

'Nothing. I was simply trying to rescue the wretched creature,' he declared in exasperation.

'From what?'

He grimaced, not caring for this cross-examination. 'A friend of mine put her on the slippery dip out at the swimming pool. She skidded down it into the water, looking very panicky. I swam over to lift her out and…'

'Dogs can swim, you know.'

'I know,' he growled. 'It was a reflex action on my part.'

'And clawing you would be a reflex action on her part. Not being able to get any purchase on the slippery dip would have terrified her.'

Another grimace at being put on the spot. 'It was only meant as a bit of fun.'

Serena raised her eyebrows, not letting him off the hook. 'Some people have strange ideas of what is fun with animals.'

'I tried to save her, remember?' He glared at the implication of cruelty. 'And let me tell you *she* wasn't the one left bleeding everywhere.'

'I'm glad to hear it. Though I think you should rearrange your thoughts on just who is the monster here. Take a good long look at whom you choose to mix with and how they treat what they consider *lesser* beings.'

The advice tripped off her tongue, pure bile on her part. He didn't like it, either, but Serena didn't care. It was about time someone got under his silver-spoon-fed, beautifully tanned, privileged skin. She was still burning over the way Lyall had discussed her with this man, telling him the kind of wife he wanted, the kind of wife he expected to get by taking on a non-competitive little hairdresser who'd be so grateful to be married to him, she'd be a perfectly compliant home-maker and never question anything he did. Definitely placing her as *a lesser being*.

But perhaps she'd gone too far on the critical front. Nic Moretti did, after all, represent one of her sister's regular clients who didn't care what it cost to keep her dog beautifully groomed—a client Michelle wouldn't like to lose. Never mind that the super-duper architect made Serena bristle from head to toe. Business was business. She stretched her mouth into an appeasing smile.

'Mrs. Gifford made a booking for Cleo at the salon this morning. If you'll fetch her for me...'

'The salon,' he repeated grimly. 'Do you cut claws there or do I have to take her to the vet?'

'We do trim pets' nails.'

'Then please do it while you've got her in *your* custody,' he growled. 'Have you got a leash for her?'

Serena raised her eyebrows. 'Doesn't Cleo have her own?'

'I'm not going near that dog until its claws are clipped.'

'Fine! I'll get one from the van.'

Unbelievable that a man of his size should be cowed by a miniature dog! Serena shook her head over the absurdity as she collected a leash and a bag of crispy bacon from the van. The latter was always a useful bribe if a dog baulked at doing what she wanted it to do. The need to show some superiority over Nic Moretti, even if it was only with a small silky terrier, burned through Serena's heart.

He waited for her by the front door, still scowling over their exchange. Or maybe he had a hangover. Clearly the ringing of the doorbell had got him out of bed and he wasn't ready to face the rest of the day yet. Serena gave him a sunny smile designed to reproach his ill humour.

'Do you want to lead me to Cleo or shall I wait here until you shoo her out of the house?'

His eyes glinted savagely at the latter suggestion, conscious of retaining some semblance of dignity, even in his boxer shorts. 'You can have the fun of catching her,' he said, waving Serena into the house.

'No problem,' she tossed at him, taking secret satisfaction in the tightening of his jaw.

Though her pulse did skip a little as she passed him by. Nic Moretti had the kind of aggressive masculinity that would threaten any woman's peace of mind. Serena tried telling herself he was probably gay. Many artistic men were. In fact, he had the mean, moody and magnificent look projected by the pin-up models in the gay calendars her former employer had lusted over in his hairdressing salon.

Mentally she could hear Ty raving on, 'Great pecs, washboard stomach, thighs to die for...'

The old patter dried up as the view in front of her claimed her interest. The foyer was like the apron of a stage, polished boards underfoot, fabulous urns dressing its wings. Two steps led down to a huge open living area where practically every piece of furniture was an ultra-modern objet d'art. Mind-boggling stuff.

Beyond it all was a wall of glass which led her gaze outside to a vast patio shaded by sails, and a luxurious spa from which a water slide—the infamous slippery dip—led to a glorious swimming pool on a lower level. She didn't see a kennel anywhere, nor the dog she'd come to collect.

She threw an inquiring glance back over her shoulder to the man in charge, only to find his gaze fastened on her derrière. Her heart skipped several beats. Nic Moretti couldn't be gay. Only heterosexual men were fascinated by the jutting contours of the well-rounded backside that had frequently embarrassed Serena by drawing wolf-whistles.

It wasn't really voluptuous. Her muscle tone was good, no dimple of cellulite anywhere. She simply had a bottom that stuck out more than most, or was more emphasised by the pit in her back. Of course, wearing shorts probably did draw more attention to it, but she saw no reason to hide the shape of her body anyway. At least the denim didn't invite the pinching she had sometimes been subjected to in the streets of Sydney while waiting for a pedestrian traffic light to change to green.

It was just her bad luck that Lyall Duncan was a *bottom* man, finding that particular piece of female equipment sexier than big breasts or long legs or whatever else men fancied in a woman. More to the point, he'd told Nic Moretti so, the memory of which instantly turned up Serena's heat level. Was he recognising *this* feature of her?

'Where might I find Cleo?' she rapped out, snapping his attention back to the business in hand.

His gaze lifted but the dark frown returned, as though he was pulling his wandering mind back from a place he found particularly vexatious. 'I don't know,' he said testily. 'I've only just rolled out of bed…'

'What do we have here?' another voice inquired, a female voice lifted in a supercilious upper class drawl.

Serena's hackles rose again. Her head whipped around. The newcomer on the scene was drifting into the open living area from what had to be a bedroom wing. She was wearing a slinky thigh-length silk and lace negligee in an oyster shade, one arm up, lazily ruffling long tawny hair. An amused little smile sat on a face that could have graced the cover of a fashion magazine, as could the rest of her, the tall slender figure being of model proportions.

'Ah…Justine…' Nic Moretti said in deep relief.

Perfect name for her, Serena thought caustically.

'…have you seen Cleo? This…uh…lady…has come to collect her for some grooming.'

He'd forgotten her name. Typical! Not important enough on his social scale to remember. Which was just as well, given other memories he might be nursing.

'Grooming!' Justine rolled her eyes. Green eyes. 'Pity she hasn't come to put the monster down. You should have let the wretched little beast drown yesterday, Nic.'

'Angelina would never forgive me if I let any harm come to her pet, Justine,' he reproved in a tight tone.

'It's obviously spoiled rotten,' came the sneering response.

'Nevertheless…'

'You'll find it shut up in the laundry,' she informed with towering distaste. 'I don't know how you could have slept through all its yap-yap-yapping outside the bedroom door last night. It was driving me mad. And the little bitch was so rabid, I had to pick it up by its collar and carry it away from me.'

Half choking it to death, Serena thought venomously.

'You should have woken me. Let me deal with it,' Nic grated out, undoubtedly aware of the cruelty to animals tag which was fast gathering more momentum.

Great company he kept! Hot body, cold mean heart. Serena viewed Justine from a mountain of contempt as she carried on like a spoiled rich bitch who expected to always be the centre of attention.

'Leaving me alone while you nurse-maided a dog? No thanks.' Her eyelids lowered in flirtatious play. 'Much better to have no distractions, wasn't it, darling?'

A clearing of throat behind Serena suggested some embarrassment. 'The laundry,' Nic Moretti growled, stepping up to her side and gesturing her to follow him. 'It's this way.'

'Watch the mess!' Justine warned. 'There's bound to be some. I threw in a leftover chicken leg to stop the yapping.'

'A chicken leg!' Serena stopped and glared at the self-serving woman. 'Cooked chicken bones splinter. They could stick in the dog's throat.'

'Let's go!' Nic muttered urgently.

He was right. This was no time to be instructing anyone. Besides which, Justine would probably rejoice if Cleo was dead. At least Nic Moretti had an anxious air about him as he led the way through a space age stainless steel kitchen.

'Cleo!' he called commandingly, striding across a mud room area containing boot racks and rows of hooks for hats, coats and umbrellas. Any thought of his own injury from Cleo's claws was apparently obliterated by the fear of injury to his sister's pet.

A shrill barking instantly started up, relieving his obvious body tension before he reached the door behind which the dog was imprisoned. He flung it open and the little silky terrier charged out between his legs, flying past Serena before she could react, shooting through the kitchen like a missile, clearly intent on escaping from any form of captivity.

'Bloody hell!' Nic breathed, glancing inside the laundry.

A determined dog was capable of creating a lot of damage. Serena didn't feel the need to comment on this. It was her job to catch Cleo who was now in the living room, barking hysterically, probably at the sight of the woman who had so callously mistreated her.

'Oh, you horrible little monster!' Justine shrieked.

Serena pelted through the kitchen just in time to see a vicious kick aimed at the silky terrier who was darting away from it. 'Cleo,' she called in a singsong tone, dropping to her knees to give herself less threatening height and tossing a piece of crispy bacon onto the floor between her and the dog.

Cleo stopped the frenetic activity, sniffed, came forward cautiously and snaffled the bacon. Serena tossed out another piece closer to herself. Then another and another as the dog responded warily to the trail being laid. Finally she snatched a piece held in Serena's fingers and paused long enough to submit to a calming scratch behind the ears. The fragile little body under its long hair was trembling—evidence of the trauma it had been through.

Serena stroked and scratched, telling Cleo in a soft indulgent tone how beautiful and clever she was until the dog was happy enough to rise up on its hind legs and lick her face.

'Oh, yuk!' Justine remarked in disgust, just as Serena scooped the dog into her arms, holding it securely against her shoulder while she rose from her kneeling position.

'Shut up, Justine!' Nic shot at her.

The classically oval jaw dropped in shock.

'Just let the lady do her job,' he expounded with no less irritation at his girlfriend's total lack of any sensitivity to the situation.

Serena almost liked him at that moment. However, she headed straight for the front door without any comment. Nic Moretti followed her right out to the van.

'What door do you want opened?' he asked solicitously.

'The driver's side. I'll put her on the passenger seat beside me so I can pat her. There's a dog harness attached to the safety belt so she won't be a problem when I'm driving.'

He opened the door and watched as Serena settled Cleo into the harness. 'She seems to be okay,' he said half anxiously.

'Fighting fit,' Serena answered dryly.

'I don't think Justine is used to dogs.'

'Maybe you should growl at her more often.' This terse piece of advice took him aback. Serena was past dealing in diplomacy. She reached out and pulled her door shut, then spoke to him through the opened window. 'Normally I would deliver Cleo back at one o'clock. How does that sit with you?'

'Fine!' He was frowning again.

'Will your girlfriend still be here?'

The dark eyes suddenly took on a rivetting intensity. His mouth thinned into a grim set of determination. 'No, she won't,' he stated categorically.

The decision gave Serena a highly pleasant sense of satisfaction. 'Then I'll see you at one o'clock.'

CHAPTER TWO

NIC MORETTI watched the van until it turned onto the public road, chagrined by the way the sassy little piece behind the driver's wheel had got under his skin, yet unable to dismiss the truths she had flung in his face. A pet groomer...obviously caring more about the canine breed than she did for people. Though he had to concede he hadn't cut too impressive a figure this morning. Justine even less so.

Which brought him to the sobering conclusion that the scorn in those vivid blue eyes had been justified and maybe it was time he took stock of what he was doing, shrugging off stuff he didn't like for the sake of cruising along in the social swim, doing his balancing act with people on the grounds that no one was perfect and if they were good for something, what did it matter if they fell short in other areas?

Judgment day...

He shook his head over the irony of that being delivered to him by a pet groomer who'd descended on him out of nowhere. Damned if he could even remember the name she had given! *Michelle* had been printed on the van she drove but he was sure it wasn't that.

And it still niggled him that he had seen her before somewhere. Though it seemed highly unlikely, given her job and location on the Central Coast. Sydney was his usual stamping ground. Besides, how could he forget that pert mouth and even perter bottom? Both of them were challenges he rather fancied coming to grips with.

He smiled self-mockingly at this last thought.

The hangover from last night's party was obviously affecting his brain. What could he possibly have in common with a pet groomer, except the welfare of Cleo for the duration of Angelina's overseas trip? Better get his mind geared to deal with Justine who was turning into a royal pain over his sister's beloved Cleo. Worse than that, in fact. There was a cruel streak in her treatment of the dog and Nic didn't like it. He wouldn't invite her here again.

He frowned over the memory of her laughing as she'd tossed her hapless victim onto the slippery dip yesterday. 'Here's company for you, Nic!' A great joke, laughing at the dog's frantic attempts to fight its way back up to the spa level against the inevitable skid into the pool. Unkind laughter.

He'd been annoyed by the whole episode, especially the painful scratches which had led him to transfer his annoyance to Cleo. Wrong! He could see that now. The pet groomer had straightened him out on quite a few areas that needed his attention. For one thing, dog-minding was not a breeze. It obviously required some expertise he didn't have.

Having resolved to take more positive action on that front, he went inside to face the problem he now had with Justine. She was in the kitchen, watching coffee brew in the percolator. While her attention was still engaged on getting a shot of caffeine, he viewed her with more critically assessing eyes.

Did he want their affair to continue? They'd been

reasonably compatible both sexually and socially, but the relationship had been more about superficial fun than deep and meaningful. He had the very definite feeling that *the fun* had just run out.

She turned around, probably having heard the front door shut and looking to check where he was. 'Ah! You've seen them off,' she said, rolling her eyes at the fuss of it all. 'Blissful peace for a while!'

'Cleo will be returned at one o'clock,' he informed her as he strolled into the kitchen and headed for the refrigerator. A couple of glasses of iced water should help clear the hangover.

'It is ridiculous to have our lives ruled by a dog!' Justine declared in exasperation. 'Why don't you put her in one of those boarding kennels, Nic? It would save all this aggravation and you'd be free to...'

'Out of the question,' he cut her off.

She swung on him, hands on hips. '*Why* is it out of the question?'

'I promised Angelina I'd take care of Cleo.'

'Boarding kennels are better equipped to look after that dog than you are.'

She was probably right, but that wasn't the point, Nic thought as he downed the first glass of water. Besides, he intended to learn how to handle Cleo better.

'Your sister need never know,' Justine argued.

'*I* would know. A promise is a promise.'

'What people don't know won't hurt them.'

He cocked a mocking eyebrow at her as he reached for the jug again. 'One of the principles by which you live?'

'It avoids trouble.'

'Oh, I don't know. Seems to me you get double the trouble when people find out what you've tried to hide from them.' He poured more water from the jug and drank again, wondering how many deceptions Justine had played with him.

She threw out her hands in frustrated appeal. 'You can't want to be tied to that cantankerous little bitch for the next two months.'

'I'll learn to get along with Cleo,' he answered blandly.

'Well, I won't!' she hurled at him, eyes flashing fury at his stubborn resistance to her plan. 'I'm not spending another night with that damned dog yapping its head off.'

'Then I suggest you pack up and leave, Justine, because the dog will be staying. With me.'

She looked gob-smacked.

He set the empty glass down on the kitchen bench. 'Best be gone before one o'clock,' he advised coldly. 'Please excuse me while I clean up the mess in the laundry which doesn't happen to have a doggy door for Cleo to go outside.'

He was at the doorway to the mud room before Justine caught her breath. 'You want *me* to go?' It was an incredulous squawk.

He paused to look back at her, feeling not one whit of warmth to soften his decision. 'What we have here, Justine, is an incompatible situation.'

'You'd put that miserable little dog ahead of me?'

'Perhaps the dog will be less miserable with you gone.'

'Oh!' She stamped her foot.

Nic sensed a wild tantrum teetering on the edge of

exploding from her. He didn't wait for it. If she followed him to the laundry, he'd hand her a bucket and suggest she clean up the result of her action in carelessly shutting Cleo in an inescapable place. That would undoubtedly send her packing in no time flat.

The pet groomer would have no problem with it but Justine...no way would she get down on her knees for a dog. Nor get her hands dirty. In fact, she obviously wanted to be treated like a pampered pet herself. Nic decided he didn't really care for that in a woman, certainly not in any long-term sense.

He wasn't followed.

By the time he had the laundry back in a tidy and pristine state, Justine had dressed, packed, and gone without favouring him with a farewell. The front door had been slammed shut on her way out, transmitting her pique at coming off second best to Cleo, and the engine of her SAAB convertible had roared down the driveway, punctuating her departure and displeasure.

Nic poured himself a coffee from the brew that had been left simmering and reflected that he could have appealed for understanding, maybe shifted Justine's attitude a little. Cleo wasn't just a *pet* to Angelina, more a surrogate child on whom she poured out all the frustrated love she couldn't give to a baby.

After years of trying to get pregnant, it had been a terrible grief to her when medical tests had revealed her husband's sperm count was so low it would be a miracle if she ever conceived. Poor Ward had been devastated, too, even going so far as to offer Angelina a divorce, knowing how set she was on having a family.

That wasn't an option to his sister. She and Ward

really did love each other. Their marriage seemed to have grown even stronger since the pressure to have a child had been erased. Ward had brought home the puppy for Angelina, a loveable little bundle of silky fur, and they both treated it like the queen of Egypt, nothing too good for their adored Cleo.

To put it in an impersonal boarding kennel... Nic shook his head. Angelina would never forgive him. *And* she'd know about it. Cleo was booked into the pet grooming salon every Monday morning. He'd forgotten about that earlier today but he knew it was written on Angelina's list of instructions. If the appointments weren't kept, no doubt *Michelle* would reveal that fact to his sister on her return.

Besides, as he'd told Justine, a promise was a promise. If she couldn't respect that, he was definitely better off having no further involvement with her, even if it meant being celibate for a couple of months. He couldn't overlook the cruel streak in her, either. The thought of it dampened any desire for more of Justine Knox. Good riddance, he thought, downing the last of the coffee.

A shower, a shave, a couple of hours' work in the room he'd designated as his office for the duration of his stay here, and he'd feel much more on top of everything when the pet groomer returned with Cleo at one o'clock.

'Aren't you beautiful now!' Michelle crowed indulgently as she ruffled Cleo's silver-grey silky hair with her fingers while giving it a last blast from the dryer. 'You look good, you smell good and you feel good.'

The dog's big brown eyes clung soulfully to

Michelle who invariably talked nonstop to each pet as she gave them whatever treatment was scheduled. Cleo had been given the lot this morning; nail trim, hair-clip, ears and eyes cleaned, shampoo, conditioner and blow-dry.

Serena reflected this was very little different to a hairdressing salon. Michelle even played background music, always soft romantic tracks to soothe any savage hearts, and she charged similar fees. Of course, it wasn't as upmarket, no stylish fittings or decorator items, just plain workbenches, open shelves, and a tiled floor that made cleaning easy.

The best thing about it, Serena decided, was the pets didn't talk back, dumping all their problems or complaints on the stylist who was expected to dish out unlimited sympathy even when it was obvious there were two sides to be considered. Not that that was the case with Cleo who was clearly an innocent victim, yet the darling little silky terrier hadn't even raised a bark since Serena had rescued her from the dark brute and his evil witch-woman.

'You can put on her pink ribbon, Serena,' Michelle instructed, having finished with Cleo and about to pick up another dog waiting for his turn to be pampered, a Maltese terrier who'd sat tamely in line like all the other pets in the salon, content to watch Michelle do her thing.

'I'm not sure Nic Moretti is going to appreciate the pink ribbon,' Serena dryly commented as she cut off an appropriate length from the roll Michelle kept on a shelf.

It earned the look of unshakeable authority. 'No pet leaves this salon without wearing a ribbon. It's the finishing touch. Cleo knows it and expects it. She'll be upset if you don't give it to her. You can tell Angelina's brother that from me. He has to consider the dog's sense of rightness or he's going to have a traumatised pet on his hands.'

When it came to dog handling her sister was a genius. Serena accepted her advice without question. But would Nic Moretti? Confronting him again stirred mixed feelings. The fear of being recognised as Lyall Duncan's belittling choice of wife had been somewhat allayed. It seemed unlikely that he would make the connection now, given the distraction of her current job. Besides, it would be interesting to see if he had got rid of his penthouse pet in the interests of properly safeguarding his sister's.

Smiling at Cleo as she tied the ribbon around her neck, she softly crooned, 'Pretty pink bow.'

The dog sprang up from the bench top and licked her chin. Starved for praise and affection, Serena concluded, and decided to add a bit more advice to her sister's when she spoke to Nic Moretti again. Her smile widened to a grin. Teach the brute a few lessons that would hopefully stick in his arrogant craw.

'I'm off now,' she called out to Michelle.

'Okay. Don't forget to pick up Muffy at Erina on the way back.'

'Will do.'

It was twenty minutes to one o'clock. As Serena took Cleo out to the van, she thought how good it was to be out of the city. Although Michelle's five acre property at Holgate wasn't exactly country, it was big enough to give a sense of real space and freedom while still being located close to the large populated areas of Gosford, Erina, Wamberal and Terrigal.

The salon was a large two-roomed shed behind the house and the parking area that served it took up quite a bit of room, but there was still plenty of land for Michelle's seven-year-old daughter to keep a pony which she rode every day after she came home from school. All in all, Serena thought her widowed older sister had done a fantastic job of setting up a business she could run while looking after Erin. Though she did seemed to have settled too much into the life of a single parent. Did the idea of getting involved in another relationship make her feel too vulnerable?

At thirty-two, Michelle was only four years older than herself, still very attractive with lovely glossy brown hair, big hazel eyes, a young pretty face and a whip-lean figure from all the physical work she did. Maybe her manless state was due to not having much opportunity to get out and meet people. Which could certainly be fixed now that Serena was here to mind her niece whenever her sister would like to go out.

On the other hand, not having a man in one's life was a lot less complicated. Maybe both she and her sister were better off on their own.

Serena pondered this dark thought as she settled Cleo in the van, then took off for the return trip to the Gifford house. Without a doubt she was starting to enjoy this complete change of lifestyle; not having to put on full make-up every day, not having to construct a hairstyle that fitted the out-there image of Ty's salon, not having to worry about wearing right up-to-date fashionable clothes, nor *compete* on any social scene. Lyall hadn't wanted her to compete with him but he'd certainly wanted her to shine amongst other women.

From now on, she simply wanted to be her own person. No putting on a show for anybody. And that included Nic Moretti. Wealth and success and good looks in a man were attractive attributes, but she wasn't about to let them influence her into not looking for what the man was like inside. Nor was she about to change herself to please him, just because he was attractive.

Well, not exactly attractive.

More loaded with sex appeal.

A woman would have to be dead not to notice.

But snobbery was not sexy at all, Serena strongly reminded herself, so she was not about to be softened up by Nic Moretti's sex appeal. In fact, it would be fun to get under his skin again, have those dark eyes burning intensely at her, make him see her as a person he couldn't dismiss out of hand.

Sweet revenge for how he'd spoken about her to Lyall.

Yes.

This was one man who definitely needed to be taught a few lessons.

CHAPTER THREE

IT WAS just on one o'clock when Serena rang the doorbell of the Gifford home. Perfect punctuality, she thought, and wondered if Nic Moretti would keep her waiting again. He had been told when she'd return. It was a matter of courtesy and respect to answer her call with reasonable promptness. No excuse not to.

She was constructing a few pertinent remarks about the value of *her* time when the door opened and there was the man facing her, all polished up and instantly sending a quiver through her heart. His black hair was shiny, his gorgeously fringed chocolate eyes were shiny, his jaw was shiny, even his tanned skin was shiny. The guy was a star in any woman's language.

He wore sparkling white shorts and a navy and white sports shirt and a smile that was whiter than both of them. Positively dazzling. 'Hello again,' he said pleasantly, causing Serena to swallow the bile she'd been building up against him.

'Hi!' she croaked, cravenly wishing she had put some effort into her own appearance. Too late now. Frantically regathering her scattered wits, she made the totally unbrilliant statement, 'Here's Cleo.'

He smiled down at the dog. 'And looking very…feminine.'

As opposed to her?

No, no, he was referring to the pink bow.

Get a grip, girl!

'I take it you've clipped her claws?' he asked.

'As much as they can be without making her bleed,' Serena managed to answer sensibly.

Her own blood was tingling as though it had been subjected to an electric charge. It was embarrassing to find herself so *taken* by him this time around. Hating the feeling of being at a disavantage, she seized on the action of detaching the leash from Cleo's collar. Retreat was the better part of valour in these tricky circumstances and the dog was now his responsibility, not hers.

Her fingers fumbled over the catch and the little silky terrier wriggled with impatience, anticipating the moment of freedom. Finally the deed was done, release completed, and Serena straightened up from her crouch, feeling flushed and fluttery, making the quite unnecessary declaration, 'She's all yours!'

Whereupon Cleo shot into the house, barking like a maniac.

Nic Moretti grimaced a kind of helpless appeal. 'What's got into her now?'

Here was opportunity handed to her on a plate and Serena found she couldn't resist asking, 'Is your girlfriend still here?'

'No. She left some hours ago,' he replied, frowning over the noisy racket inside the house.

'Well, I'd say Cleo is checking everywhere for her presence.'

The frown deepened. 'I think I might need some help. Would you mind coming in for a few minutes?'

He stepped back, waving her forward.

Serena hesitated, not liking the sense of having her services taken for granted just because she'd helped beyond the call of duty this morning. Being *used* by this man did not appeal to her. She wasn't his dogs-body and she certainly didn't intend to give him any cause to see her in that role.

She folded her arms in strongly negative body language. 'Mr. Moretti…'

'Nic.' A quick apologetic smile. 'I'm sorry. I didn't catch your name this morning.'

'Serena.' Which shouldn't ring any bells because Ty had decided Rene was a more fashionable name for her and Lyall had always used it, having first met her at Ty's salon where he regularly had his hair cut, styled and streaked to complement his yuppie image. 'Serena Fleming,' she added so she wasn't just a one name person. 'And I have to pick up another pet…'

'Please…' He was distracted by the shrill yapping, now in the living room behind him. It stopped abruptly, just as he glanced back at the dog. 'Oh, my God!'

He was off at a fast stride, leaving Serena standing at the door. Curiosity got the better of her earlier inclination to get out of here and away from an attraction that made her feel uncomfortable. Besides which, he had invited her in. She stepped into the foyer. On the polished floorboards of the living-room floor, precisely where the evil witch-woman had aimed a kick at Cleo this morning, was a large spreading puddle.

The dog stood back from it, wagging her tail triumphantly. Serena rolled her eyes, thinking she should have walked Cleo on the lawn before ringing the doorbell. From the kitchen came the sound of taps running full blast. Nic Moretti reappeared with a bucket and sponge.

'Why would she do that?' he demanded in exasperation. 'She knows where the doggy door is and has been trained to use it.'

'Primal instinct can be stronger than any training,' Serena dryly observed. 'Cleo has just reclaimed her territory from the enemy.'

'The enemy?' He looked totally lost.

'I'd say that's where your girlfriend's scent was the strongest. It's now been effectively killed.'

'Right!' He gritted his teeth, bent down and proceeded to sponge up the puddle.

His thighs bulged with muscular strength. His shorts tightened across a very sexy butt. From her elevated position in the stepped up foyer, Serena couldn't help smiling at the view of this magnificent male, almost on his hands and knees, performing a menial task that a woman was usually expected to do. Her feeling of inferiority evaporated.

'See what I mean?' he grumbled. 'I have a problem.'

'It is easily fixable,' Serena blithely assured him. 'You're doing a good job there.'

'This is only one thing.' He looked up, caught her amused smile and huffed his frustration at the position he was in. 'Obviously I need a dog psychologist to explain why Cleo is running amok.'

'Well, you can always contact the television show, *Harry's Practice,* and see if you can line up a visit.'

'From everything you've said, *you're* the person I want,' he declared, dropping the sponge into the bucket and straightening up to his full height to eye her with commanding intensity.

Serena couldn't deny a little thrill at his *wanting*

her, even if it was only in an advisory capacity.
Which would put her on top in this relationship. The
boss. A very tempting situation. Except she couldn't
bring herself to pretend she was something she
wasn't.

'I'm not a qualified dog psychologist.'

'But you know how dogs think. And react,' he
bored in.

'More or less,' she replied offhandedly, half turning
towards the front door as she realised he was grasping
at what he saw as the *easy* option. He didn't *want*
her. He wanted to make use of her, which placed her
as his servant, and she was not about to become his
willing slave. 'I really do have to go now,' she tossed
at him. 'Muffy's owner is expecting me to…'

'Wait! I'll pay you.'

Typical, thinking money could buy him anything.
Serena steeled herself against giving in. 'I have a
schedule to keep. If you'll excuse me…'

'When do you finish work today?' he shot at her.

That gave her pause for second thoughts. She eyed
him consideringly. 'What do you have in mind?'

'If you could give me the benefit of your expertise
for an hour or so…'

'You're asking for a consultation?'

He seized the idea of a professional appointment.
'Yes. I'll pay whatever fee you nominate.'

An edge of desperation had crept into his voice.
Serena did some swift calculation. An hour's work on
a client's hair in Ty's salon would usually cost well
over a hundred dollars. But she had been an expert
stylist with years of training behind her. As far as
canine behavioural science was concerned, she was

strictly an amateur. But Nic Moretti didn't know that and being cheap did not engender respect.

'Seventy dollars an hour,' she decided.

'Fine!' He didn't even blink at the fee. 'Can you come this evening?'

A bit of power dressing was called for in these circumstances. Not to mention a shower, shampoo and blow-dry in order to look properly professional. 'Does seven-thirty suit?'

'Great!' he said with a huge air of relief.

The guy had to be really desperate, Serena thought, feeling positively uplifted at the idea of being the font of all wisdom to him. And she'd better arm herself with a stack of practical wisdom from Michelle this afternoon so he'd think the consultation was worth every cent of that outrageous fee.

Flashing him a brilliant smile to assure him all was well between them, she raised her hand in a farewell salute. 'Must be off. I'll be back at seven-thirty.'

Deal closed.

Very much in *her* favour.

More sweet satisfaction.

Nic watched her jaunty walk to the front door, his gaze automatically fastening on the sexy roll of the delectable twin globes of her highly female bottom, pouched pertly in the tight denim shorts. He grinned in the triumphant belief he'd just won this round with the cheeky Miss Serena Fleming. Her brain was his to pick tonight and maybe—just maybe—she'd unbend enough to let him explore the possibility of enjoying more of her than the workings of her mind.

She pulled the front door shut behind her, cutting

off the visual pleasure of her back view. Nic, however, had no problem recalling it. Her front view, as
well, the firm roundness of her breasts, emphasised
by her folded arms as she'd stood her ground and
denied him any more of her time. No favours from
Miss Fleming.

It was quite clear she disapproved of him—not the
usual response he got from women—and despite his
putting his best foot forward to make up for this
morning's fiasco, she hadn't intended to budge from
her stance. Not until he'd offered payment for her
expertise. He suspected she'd done him in the eye
there, too, demanding top dollar. Probably thought he
wouldn't agree to it.

The money was irrelevant.

He'd picked up her challenge and forced her to
come to his party. The sense of winning put Nic in
such a good mood, he even grinned down at the troublesome terrier who had brought him no pleasure at
all to this date. 'You might be good for something
after all, Cleo,' he said whimsically.

The stumpy tail wagged eager agreement.

Then Nic remembered having to clean up the puddle and he wagged an admonishing finger at the dog.
'But you certainly don't deserve that pretty pink bow.
What self-respecting female would let her bladder
loose in the wrong place?'

The accusing tone instantly broke their brief understanding. A series of hostile barks reminded Nic
that hostility bred hostility and he couldn't blame the
dog for wanting to get rid of Justine's smell. 'Okay,
okay,' he soothed, copying the soft, singsong lilt
Serena had used to calm the beast. 'You probably did

me a favour there, too, bringing out the worst of her character for me to see. Let's call it quits on Justine.'

Back to tail wagging.

'It's time for lunch now.' If any of his friends ever heard him talking to a dog like this, he'd never hear the end of it. However, it was definitely a winning ploy, so he continued in the same soppy vein. 'Would you like some more chicken?'

Chicken, according to Angelina, was a magic word that could winkle her darling pet out of any bad mood. It hadn't produced the desired result while Justine had been present, but right now it worked like a charm. Cleo literally bounced out to the kitchen and stood in front of the refrigerator, yipping impatiently for her treat.

Nic obliged, carefully deboning the chicken as he filled her food dish. She wolfed it all down, moved on to her water dish, took a long drink, then happily trotted off to her miniature trampoline in the living room, hopped onto it, scratched it into shape, curled herself down and closed her eyes in sleepy contentment.

Nic shook his head in bemusement. Maybe he didn't need Serena Fleming's advice after all. Maybe he'd only needed to get rid of Justine. On the other hand, one little success did not guarantee peaceful coexistence for two months. And something had to be done about the barking at night.

He knew Angelina and Ward let Cleo sleep on their bed. They actually laughed about it burrowing up between them. No way was he about to start sleeping with a dog, waking up to a lick on the face. Devotion to duty only went so far. And if he managed to get

Serena Fleming into bed with him, he certainly didn't want a jealous dog leaping into the fray.

Wondering if he could persuade the feisty little blonde into being his playmate for the next two months, Nic went back to the refrigerator to see what he could rustle up for his own lunch. His appetite for tasty morsels had been aroused. He spotted a bottle of Chardonnay and thought he might begin tonight's consultation by offering a glass of wine—a friendly, hospitable thing to do.

The idea of killing two birds with one stone had fast-growing appeal.

A desirable woman in his bed.

An expert dog-handler on tap.

Definitely a challenge worth winning.

CHAPTER FOUR

'SEVENTY dollars!' Michelle looked her disbelief.

'Well, I don't believe in undercharging,' Serena explained. 'It's a matter of psychology.'

'Psychology?'

'Yes. The more you make people pay, the more they believe they're getting something special. Ty taught me that.'

The disbelief took on a sceptical gleam. 'And what's the something special you're going to give Nic Moretti for his seventy dollars?'

'That's where you come in. I need all the tips you can give me on solving problems with dogs. And I'll go you halves on the fee.'

Michelle sighed at the offer. 'Well, I won't say no, but I think you might be putting yourself at risk, Serena.'

'How…if I'm all prepared?'

'I'm just remembering something Angelina Gifford said about her brother. She was expecting Cleo to adore him because there wasn't a female alive who didn't l…u…u…u…v Nic.'

'No way am I going to be a victim on that count,' Serena emphatically assured her sister. 'I'm simply fleecing the guy for being as arrogant as Lyall Duncan. Though I will play fair by giving him value for his money.'

'Hmm…he's got to you already. You've just been

hurt by one rich, eligible bachelor. Better watch your step with…'

'Michelle! I don't even like him!'

'He's striking sparks in you. That's more danger-ous than *like*.'

'Oh, for goodness' sake! It's just a one-hour deal. And I need your help.'

'Okay. Let's see if you can keep your mind on the job.'

I am not going to let Nic Moretti close enough to hurt me, Serena silently vowed. Her sister didn't un-derstand the score. This was simply a game of one-upmanship where she ended up the winner.

For the rest of the afternoon, her mind was trained on collecting all the advice that would make Nic Moretti's head spin with her bank of expert knowl-edge. Admiration, respect, gratitude…that was what she wanted from him. Balm for her wounded pride.

And, of course, it was pride behind the care she took with her appearance that evening. Not that she went all out to impress in any sexual sense. No per-fume. No jewellery. No eye make-up. Only some per-fectly applied pink lipstick. Her hair was newly clean and shiny and she left it long and loose, except for the side tresses which were held together at the back with a clip to maintain a neat, tidy effect.

Deciding on smart casual clothes, she teamed tur-quoise blue slacks with a tailored white shirt sprinkled with pink and turquoise and purple daisies. She strapped a businesslike navy Swatch watch on her wrist, pushed her feet into navy sandals and picked up a small navy shoulderbag to hold her keys and

money. With this outfit, no one, not even her too per-
ceptive older sister, could say she was man-hunting.

Michelle and Erin were settled in the lounge room,
like two peas in a pod with their light brown hair cut
in short bobs, their delicately featured faces recognis-
ably mother and daughter, and both of them dressed
in blue jeans and red T-shirts. Serena waved to them
from the doorway. 'I'm off now.'

'You look pretty, Aunty Serena,' her niece remarked.

'Good enough to eat,' Michelle dryly added.
'Watch out for big bad wolves!'

'Oh, Mummy!' Erin chided, giggling at the reference to a fairy story. 'She's not wearing a red cape
and hood.'

'Besides, I'm wolf-proof,' Serena declared.

But she wasn't quite so sure of that when Nic
Moretti invited her into his lair twenty minutes later.
He suddenly looked very wolfish in tight black jeans
and an open-necked white shirt which played peek-a-
boo with the sprinkle of black curls that had been
fully displayed on the centre of his chest this morning,
reminding Serena of what else had been displayed.

Fortunately, Cleo was also at the door to greet her.
She bent down to scratch the little terrier behind her
ears, sealing an easy bond of affection between them
while sternly reminding herself that the dog had to be
the focus of her attention here, regardless of how *distracting* Nic Moretti was. However, as she straightened up, the top button of her shirt popped out of its
buttonhole, giving the man of the moment a tunnel
vision shot of cleavage.

Which he took.

Completely destroying the sense of starting this encounter on a professional footing.

Serena sighed with frustration, inadvertently causing her breasts to lift, pushing the opening further apart. Embarrassed, she clutched the edges of the shirt and hauled them back together.

'Excuse me. This new cotton stretch fabric obviously has its perils,' she bit out, shoving the button back in its hole and fiercely hoping it would stay there.

Nic Moretti lifted a twinkling gaze that elevated the heat in her bloodstream. 'That button would have to be classified as a sexual tease,' he said, amusement curling through his voice.

'It's not meant to be,' she flashed back at him.

'Perhaps it's better left open. The temptation to watch for it to pop again might get beyond my control.'

'This is ridiculous!' Serena muttered, fighting against losing her own control of the situation. 'Why are you flirting with me?'

He laughed. 'Because it's fun. Can't you enjoy some fun, Serena?'

'This is a professional visit,' she hotly insisted.

His eyes teased her attempt at seriousness. 'Does that mean you have to keep yourself buttoned up?'

'Oh, puh-lease!' Anger at his lack of respect flared. 'If you're going to be impossible, let's call this consultation off right now!'

Cleo yapped at the sudden burst of temper from her.

'Sorry, sorry.' Nic's hand shot up in a halting gesture as he made a valiant attempt to reconstruct his expression into apologetic appeal. 'Just a touch light-headed from the relief of having you come.'

She wrenched her gaze from the lurking twinkle in his and looked down at the agitated dog. 'It's okay,' she soothed. 'As long as your keeper behaves him-self.'

'She's been very good this afternoon. No trouble at all,' Nic said in a straight tone.

'Then you don't need me.'

'Yes, I do,' came the quick retort, the vehement tone drawing her gaze back to his. The dark eyes were now burning with an intensity of purpose that would not be denied. 'The nights are bad. Very bad. Come…I'll show you.'

He gestured her to fall into step with him. Relieved they were getting down to proper business, Serena moved forward, traversing the foyer to the living room with a determinedly confident walk, though feeling oddly small and all too vulnerable with her head only level to his big broad shoulders. She wasn't petite. In fact, she was above average height for a woman. It was just that he was very tall. And strong. And terribly macho looking, which was probably due to his Italian heritage.

Nevertheless, her heart was racing.

She was acutely conscious of being alone in this house with this man, not that she believed he would really come onto her but that initial bit of flirting had been deeply unsettling, making her aware that he found her attractive. Maybe even desirable.

While that was very flattering—and ironic, since he'd criticised Lyall for choosing her as his mate for marriage—Serena wished Nic Moretti wasn't quite so sexually desirable himself. He was much more of a *hunk* than Lyall, whose luxurious lifestyle and lavish romancing had seduced her into thinking herself in love with him. Which, she realised now, wasn't the same as being *hot* for him.

Every nerve in her body jangled alarm as Nic cupped her elbow to steer her towards what she had assumed this morning was the bedroom wing. 'Where are we going?' she demanded suspiciously.

'To view the damage so you'll understand what I'm dealing with,' he answered reasonably.

'Okay. Damage,' she agreed unhitching her elbow from his grasp.

He cocked an eyebrow at the somewhat graceless action. 'Do you have a thing about personal space?'

'Only when it's invaded without my giving a green light.'

'I'll remember that,' he said with a quirky little smile. 'If you're still nervous about that button…'

'I am not nervous!' she hotly denied, barely stopping herself from looking down to check that it was still fastened.

Cleo yapped again, apparently keeping a barometer on her temperature level.

'Fine!' Nic said with too much satisfaction for Serena's comfort. 'I'd much prefer you to feel relaxed.'

They were now walking down a wide curved corridor. On its south side, floor length windows gave a view of fern-filled courtyards. Closed doors along the other wall obviously led to bedrooms with their windows facing north, getting all-day sunshine and the spectacular vista of shoreline and sea.

'Where's the damage?' Serena asked, totally unable to relax her inner tension.

Nic pointed ahead to the door at the end of the corridor. 'That leads to the master bedroom suite. The first night I was here alone with Cleo, she barked continually outside that door. I showed her no one was in the suite, then took her back to her trampoline. It didn't stop her. She returned and…see for yourself…attacked the door, scratching to get in.'

'I take it Mr. and Mrs. Gifford allowed her to sleep on their bed.'

'Yes, but I thought with them gone…' He sighed. 'In the end, I let her in and left her there.'

'Problem solved?'

He grimaced. 'It only worked the first night. The second night she attacked my door. See?'

Scratches on the second door.

'She wanted to sleep with someone,' Serena interpreted.

'I am not having a dog in bed with me,' Nic growled.

'She's only little.' It was more a tease than an argument, the words popping out of Serena's mouth before she could think better of them.

The comment earned a blistering glare. 'Do you ever reach a climax?'

'I beg your pardon?'

'I can't imagine how your boyfriend manages to get you to a sufficient level of excitement if you have a dog interfering all the time.'

'I don't have a boyfriend,' she flared at him.

'Not surprising if you insist on sleeping with a third party.'

'I don't have a dog, either!'

'So why load me with one in my bed?'

'You told me your girlfriend was gone,' Serena hurled back at him, getting very hot under the collar, so hot her tongue made the unwise move of fanning the flames. 'I didn't know you had another *third party* waiting in the wings.'

His eyes sizzled back at her, lifting the heat to furnace level. 'Sometimes unexpected things happen,' he drawled. 'Have we now established that neither you nor I want a dog in bed with us?'

'There is no…*us,*' Serena hissed, completely losing her head.

'Of course there is. Here we are together…'

'In consultation!'

'Absolutely! And very interesting it is, too.'

'So let's get back to Cleo,' she shot out, desperate to get both their minds off *bed*. 'After she barked and scratched at this door, what did you do?'

'Got up, watched television, fell asleep on the chaise longue in the living room.'

'Then let's go back to the living room.'

She swung on her heel and did some fast power-walking out of the bedroom wing which was far too sensitive a place to be with a man who oozed sexual invitation.

'So, the second night you spent out here on…' Her gaze swung around and fastened on the only piece of furniture that remotely resembled a chaise longue. 'Do you mean that spiky blue thing?'

It looked like more of an instrument of torture than a place to sleep. A round stainless steel base with a central cylinder supported a curved lounger shape covered with dozens of protruding blue cones which certainly looked too sharp to lie on comfortably.

Nic grinned. 'It's a fantastic design. The cones are made of a specially developed flexible rubber foam. They wrap around your body and let you submerge into them. And they're temperature sensitive, reacting to your body heat, sinking down to cushion and support anyone's individual shape.'

Serena shook her head in amazement.

'Try it for yourself,' Nic urged, waving her forward as he moved forward himself.

Curiosity drew her to the savage looking piece of furniture. 'I've never seen anything like it,' she remarked, still with a sense of disbelief in its comfort.

'It's a prototype. Not on the market yet. It's currently being displayed in international furniture shows,' Nic explained. 'Ward, Angelina's husband, likes to showcase the latest designs. He supplies to interior decorators.'

She hadn't known what business the Giffords were in but this information certainly made sense of their space age decor. 'Well, I guess you could say the chaise longue is spectacular, but I am reminded of a porcupine.'

'Don't be put off. Sit on the concave section, then swivel onto the back rest as you swing your legs up.'

The construction was so extraordinary Serena couldn't resist testing it, though once she was fully stretched out on the cones, the experience was so incredibly sensual, it made her terribly aware of her body, especially with Nic Moretti standing over her, smiling as he watched the chaise longue adjust to her shape and length.

His gaze travelled down her legs and back again, lingering at the apex of her thighs, almost making her squirm. He made another pause at the precarious button…willing it to pop? Serena felt her nipples tightening, pushing at the flimsy fabric of her bra. Her body heat was accelerating so fast, it would probably melt the seductive cones if she didn't get off.

She jackknifed back to a sitting position, swinging her feet firmly onto the floor again. 'Okay…' He was standing too close. Her eyes stabbed at his, demanding he give her more room as she determinedly switched her mind to business. 'Where was Cleo while you slept here?'

A tantalising little smile played on his lips as he backed off and gestured to a small dog's trampoline bed, set between two weirdly curved chairs facing a huge television screen. Obviously this was Cleo's place when the Giffords watched their favourite programs.

'She's in the habit of sleeping there when it suits her,' Nic said wryly. 'Apparently it doesn't suit her at night unless I'm out here with her. I was hoping when Justine arrived on Saturday…but no.' He heaved a much put upon sigh. 'Once again I ended up on the chaise longue because Cleo was driving us mad.'

Justine would have loved that—distracted from sexual pleasure, then deserted for a dog. No doubt there'd been premeditated murder in her heart when she'd put the little terrier on the slippery dip for a fast slide into deep water. Serena smiled at Cleo, silently congratulating the dog for frustrating Justine and being the survivor. Its tail wagged in conspiratorial satisfaction. Serena decided she could become very fond of Cleo, clearly a cunning intelligence at work in that little brain.

'I had a party of friends here yesterday,' Nic went on. 'By the time they left, I fell into bed and...' He grimaced. 'Well, you know how Justine dealt with last night.'

Serena looked him straight in the eye. 'Not a kind solution.'

'No,' he agreed, then pointedly added, 'My relationship with Justine came to an abrupt end this morning.'

Exit the witch-woman...enter the dog-handler?

His eyes held a gleam that told Serena he definitely fancied her as a replacement. It was a highly purposeful and suggestive gleam, reinforcing all the suggestive stuff he'd thrown at her outside his bedroom door.

While her mind furiously resented his assumption that she would share this desire, her body had a will of its own, seriously responding with little charges of electric excitement running riot everywhere. The heat coursing through her completely dried up her mouth and throat. It rose to her brain, as well, and wiped out any sensible thought processes. The only words forming there were, *I want you, too.*

Which, of course, was mad, reckless, shocking and inadmissable. The silence stretched into a seething mass of unspeakable words...

Why shouldn't I experience him?

He's free.

He's gorgeous, sexy, and I've never felt this physically attracted to anyone in my whole life.

The voice of caution finally kicked in…

It won't lead anywhere,

Remember his snobby attitudes.

He just wants to use you while he's stuck here.

You'll get involved and end up hurt.

Her body started screaming a positively wanton protest…

Don't think pain. Think pleasure.

This could be the best you'll ever have!

Fortunately Nic broke the wild torrent inside her by speaking himself. 'I was going to offer you a drink when you arrived.' He smiled in self-reproach. 'Got sidetracked. Will you have one with me now?'

'Yes,' she croaked. Her mouth was a desert.

He led off to the kitchen. She followed slowly on legs that had gone slightly wobbly on her. By the time she reached the kitchen he had wineglasses set on a bench and was pouring from a chilled bottle of Chardonnay that he'd obviously opened and re-corked earlier. A premeditated tactic for seduction?

Serena told herself she should protest. She was driving and this was supposed to be a professional consultation. No alcohol. But her gravel throat needed an instant injection of liquid so when he handed her a glass, she took it and sipped, silently vowing not to drink much.

'Thank you.' Even with the soothing moisture of the wine her voice was still husky. She drank some more.

'You like it?' he asked.

'Nice oaky flavour,' she answered, not to be out-done on the wine-tasting front. Nic Moretti might mix with high society in Sydney, but she wasn't exactly a backwoods girl to be patronised by him or any-one else.

He raised an amused eyebrow. 'You're an expert on Chardonnay, too?'

'I have many talents,' she said loftily and deliber-ately left him guessing as she returned to the one he was paying her for. 'Since you don't want Cleo in your bed...'

His eyes said he infinitely preferred *her* between his sheets.

'...and you don't want her keeping you awake all night...'

'Please don't say I have to camp permanently on the chaise longue,' he appealed.

Not big enough for two, putting a severe constric-tion on his sex life, Serena thought, though a wicked afterthought fancied it could provide some interesting sensations. She dragged her wayward mind back to the business in hand.

'No. But we do have to create a secure and com-fortable environment for her with no access to the bedroom wing. I presume there is a doggy door for her to get in and out?'

'The mud room.'

'Can this room be closed off from the rest of the house?'

'Yes,' he breathed in huge relief. 'It's just through here.'

They moved from the kitchen to the mud room which Serena had briefly seen this morning. She checked out the doggy door, then viewed the rows of hooks on the wall.

'I think they're too high to hang blankets from,' she decided.

'Blankets?'

'What I'd recommend is a kind of cage to throw blankets over at night. You put the trampoline bed inside and make it a snuggly place for Cleo so she'll feel safe.' She nodded to the corner where only an easily removable umbrella stand was in the way. 'That corner would be best.'

'The bar stools could make a cage.' Having seized the idea, he moved into action. 'I'll go and get them. Blankets, too.'

Relieved of the influence his magnetic presence had on her, Serena took a long, deep breath and tried to figure out what she should do about Nic Moretti. Before the hour was up a decision had to be made. Yes or no. Hold the line here or let it be pushed further.

She remembered her sister relating Angelina Gifford's words… *There wasn't a female alive who didn't love Nic.* So getting any woman he wanted was all too easy.

The idea of being *easy* for him did not appeal.

It smacked of being one of a queue lining up to serve his pleasure. Never mind that her pleasure might be served, too. Pride insisted that he would value her more if she played hard to get.

But then she might lose her chance.

Well, if she lost it she lost it, Serena finally reasoned. After her experience with Lyall Duncan, she wanted to be valued as the person she was, not considered just another roll in the hay, suiting Nic Moretti's convenience.

To be viewed—taken—like that would be too demeaning.

Humiliating.

The decision had to be no.

The plain truth was she was off her brain to even consider having any kind of relationship with Nic Moretti. How could she ever feel good about it, knowing what she knew about him and his attitudes?

Give it up right now.

Right now! she repeated to stamp it in her mind.

CHAPTER FIVE

NIC returned to the mud room, carrying a bar stool heaped with blankets. He grinned at her. 'If this works, I'll have a cage frame made tomorrow.'

The grin played havoc with Serena's resolution. Warm pleasure zinged from him, making her skin tingle and her toes curl. She found herself clutching her wineglass too tightly and realised she was still holding it. Nic had set his down somewhere.

He put the stool in the corner she'd indicated. 'Won't be long bringing the others,' he tossed at her and strode off through the doorway to the kitchen again, leaving Serena to catch her breath.

The guy was dynamite, especially when he was being charming. She gulped down some of the Chardonnay in the hope it would cool her down. A console table with a mirror above it stood near the entrance to the kitchen. She set her glass on it and checked her reflection in the mirror.

Her cheeks were almost as pink as her lipstick and her eyes were fever bright, vividly blue. Her hair was slightly mussed from lying on the porcupine chaise longue and she quickly smoothed it back and refastened the clip. It made her feel slightly more *together,* instead of in danger of falling apart.

While Nic brought the other three stools, Cleo trotted back and forth with him, intrigued by all this strange activity. Serena concentrated on keeping out

of his way, unfolding the blankets and figuring out
how best to construct the cave for the troublesome
little terrier.

Once Nic had finished his task, he closed in on her
again, assisting with the blanket spreading. Desperate
to avoid even accidental contact, which Serena feared
might lead to purposeful contact, she sent him off on
another mission.

'We need a radio.'

He gave her a quizzical look. 'What do we need a
radio for?'

'Company for Cleo.'

'Company?'

'She won't feel she's alone if a radio is playing.
You can set it on the console table over there. I saw
a power-point next to it.'

'I'm to leave a radio playing all night?' he queried.

'If you turn the volume down low, you shouldn't
hear it from the bedroom wing.'

He went off, shaking his head and muttering, 'I
can't believe I'm doing this for a dog.'

Serena smiled and her inner tension relaxed a little.
The *pro temps* cave was as secure as she could make
it by the time Nic returned with a very expensive
looking radio. He looked sternly at the dog at his feet
as he set it on the console table. 'I hope you appreciate I'm giving this up for you.'

Cleo yipped her appreciation.

'Best you tune it into a station now so you can just
switch it on later,' Serena advised. 'Find one that
plays classical music.'

Nic gave her an incredulous look. 'Are you telling

me dogs know the difference between Beethoven and
Britney Spears?'

'Which music would you prefer to go to sleep
with?'

'Now there's an interesting question.' Wicked
speculation sparkled at her. 'What turns you on...or
off...as the case may be? Violins, guitar, tom-toms...'

'I doubt Cleo will settle down to a jungle beat,'
Serena cut in with pointed emphasis on the terrier.
'Excessive drumming might well set her barking.'

'Right! Soft, soothing music.' He fiddled until he
found it, gave Serena a smugly triumphant look, then
declared, 'Now we can put Cleo to bed.'

'Absolutely not,' Serena corrected him. 'You can't
do that until you're ready to go yourself.'

His lashes lowered, barely veiling a look of searing
intent that put a host of butterflies in her stomach.
Bed was definitely on his mind, but not in the context
of sleeping. She could almost hear him thinking, *I'm
ready if you are.*

'Cleo won't settle while ever she senses anyone is
still up and around,' Serena rushed out, clutching
frantically at any defence—including the active presence of Cleo—to keep Nic Moretti at arm's length.
'Putting her in here is the last thing you do at night,'
she stated emphatically. 'And there are other things
you should do, as well.'

'Like what?' he bit out with an air of sorely tried
patience.

Three doors led out of the mud room, one to the
kitchen, one to the laundry, and the third she assumed
to a corridor that served another wing of the house.

'Mostly Cleo would come into this room via the kitchen, wouldn't she?'

'Yes.'

'I suggest you bring her in that way, with her trampoline bed which you'll set in the makeshift cave. Then turn the radio on, lay a big pillow along the bottom of the closed kitchen door...'

'A pillow?'

'To stop her from scratching at a familiar exit,' Serena explained matter-of-factly, trying to ignore the increased charge of electricity coming from him. 'You can go out the other door once you settle her into the cave.'

'Is that all?' Nic drawled, clearly wanting to move on to other scenarios which had nothing to do with canine behaviour.

Serena had to concede, 'All I can think of at the moment.'

'Good!' He picked up her wineglass which she'd emptied and set aside earlier. His grin came back in full force, barrelling into her heart and dizzying her brain. 'Let's go and raise a toast to the success of this plan. Plenty of wine left in the bottle.'

She was drawn into accompanying him back into the kitchen where he headed for the refrigerator to extract the bottle of Chardonnay. Wine was an intoxicant she certainly didn't need with Nic Moretti scrambling any straight thinking, though at least it would keep his hands occupied for a little while, Serena reasoned, and she didn't have to drink much. A quick check of her watch showed the hour was almost up. She only had to get through another ten minutes.

'You must live locally,' he said as he refilled their glasses.

'Yes.'

'Where?'

'Holgate.'

'Been there all your life?'

Alarm bells rang. Was he trying to *place* her again, a memory of her still niggling? 'It's a good place to be,' she answered evasively, then quickly returned a question which established the distance she knew was between them. 'You're usually based in Sydney, aren't you?'

'Yes. I have an apartment at Balmoral.'

North Shore million dollar territory. Serena privately bet his apartment was in a prime position overlooking Sydney Harbour. The best of everything for Nic Moretti.

He handed her the filled glass, his eyes twinkling suggestively as he added, 'But I'll be supervising a project near Gosford so I'll be commuting quite a bit until it's completed.'

He was holding out the bait that he'd be available for longer than the two months his sister and brother-in-law were away. Serena didn't believe for one moment there was a chance in hell that he'd pursue a serious relationship with her. On the social scale, a dog-handler was probably a rung down from a hairdresser. The trick was to keep him talking so he didn't zero in on her.

'I saw photos of your sketches for the park in the local newspaper. Very impressive.' She lifted her glass in a toast to his talent. 'Should be a great place to go in the future.'

'Thank you.' He looked surprised at her knowledge but the light of golden opportunity swiftly followed surprise. 'I'm pleased with the plan. Would you like to see more of it? I have it here. I've turned one of the bedrooms into a temporary office.'

No way was she going near the bedroom wing again! Her heart was galloping at the idea of sharing the intimacy of looking at his designs. The temptation to share even deeper intimacies would be hanging in the air, gathering momentum the whole time.

Stay cool, she commanded herself, forcefully overriding the strong inclination to say *yes*.

Just smile and decline.

'Perhaps another time. I must be off soon. I have family waiting for me. Do you have other problems with Cleo you'd like to discuss before I go?'

He frowned, probably at his failure to seduce her into falling in with *his* plan of action. 'The nights have been the worst. She was okay this afternoon with just having me here.'

Serena nodded wisely. 'A party of strangers would have been unsettling for her.'

'I guess so.' He grimaced at the reminder, then clinked Serena's glass with his and smiled, pouring out another dose of sexually charged charm. 'We were going to drink to the success of your advice.'

'I hope it works for you,' Serena replied, very sincerely, given the fee she'd demanded. She took a sip of the wine, battling the effect of his smile which had stirred a hornet's nest of hormones, then determinedly set the glass on the bench beside her. 'If there's nothing else…?'

With an air of reluctant resignation, he took out his wallet and handed her the seventy dollars.

'Thank you.' She tucked the money into her shoulder bag, pointedly getting her car keys out at the same time, then gave him her best smile to soften the ego blow of her departure. 'I can be contacted at Michelle's Pet Grooming Salon should you need any more help.'

'Fine!' His dark eyes suddenly glittered with the determination to take up a challenge. 'I'll see you to your car.'

Proximity was definitely dangerous. Serena seized on *the third party* to protect her from whatever Nic Moretti had in mind. 'Then I suggest you bring Cleo along. Take her for a walk on the lawn. I saw her leash hanging up in the mud room.'

The glitter turned to a sizzle. He looked down at the dog who was sitting on the kitchen floor watching both of them. More than likely it was going to follow where they went and he'd be stuck with a fuss at the front door if he tried to close her inside. Muttering something dark and dire under his breath, he went to the mud room, Cleo trailing after him, and he secured the leash on her before reappearing, the dog in tow.

'Ready!' he declared through gritted teeth.

Cleo yipped excitedly.

'Walkies for you,' Serena crooned at her, laughing inside as she went ahead of them, out of the kitchen, through the living room, up to the foyer.

She wasn't aware that her bottom was swinging in jaunty triumph at having won this round with Nic Moretti, nor that it was being viewed with a burning desire to have it clutched hard in the hands of the man who was following her. Clutched and lifted so her body fitted snugly to the rampant need she had aroused.

She paused at the front door and he quickly reached around her to open it. A whiff of tantalisingly male aftershave cologne caught in her nostrils. On top of all his other sexy attributes, he even smelled good. It put Serena on pins and needles as she stepped outside and headed for her car, a neat little Peugeot 360 which always gave her the sense of welcoming her into it. She needed that tonight. A safe refuge from the big bad wolf.

He walked beside her, emanating a tension that robbed her of any conversational train of thought. He didn't say anything for her to hit off, either. Cleo was trotting in front of them. They'd reached the driver's side of the car when the little terrier suddenly stopped, then darted back around Serena's legs, tripping her up with the leash. She stumbled in her haste to step over it and found herself scooped against a hard unyielding chest.

'I'm okay,' she gasped, her hands curling at the body heat coming through his shirt.

'You're shaking,' he said, his arm encircling her even more firmly, bringing her into such acute physical contact with him, it set off tremors that had nothing to do with almost losing her balance.

She looked up in agitated protest. The blazing intensity of his eyes so close to hers had a hypnotic force that fried her brain, turning her into a passive dummy as he slowly lowered his head towards her upturned face. Even with more intimate collision imminent, she couldn't bring herself to react. His mouth covered hers and then it was too late to think, to speak, to do anything but feel him.

His lips seemed to tug at hers, enticing them to open, though there was no blitzing invasion, more a slow, sensual exploration that had her whole mouth tingling with excitement, his tongue teasing, goading, twining. She was drawn into actively participating, compelled to respond by a need to know more, feel more.

Whether this signalled consent or surrender, Serena had no idea. Her mind was flooded with intoxicating sensation. Yet what had been enthralling suddenly exploded into wild passion and a tidal wave of chaotic need crashed through her entire body, engulfing her with such power she completely lost herself in it, craving hot and urgent union with the man who was kissing her, holding her locked to him.

Her thighs clung to the strong muscularity of his, revelling in their maleness. Her stomach exulted in the questing erection that pressed into it. Her breasts wantonly flattened themselves against the heated wall of his chest, instinctively seeking the beat of his heart. Her arms wound around his neck, as fiercely possessive as the hands curled around her bottom, lifting her into this fantastic fit with him.

She was consumed with excitement, the rampant desire coursing between them blotting out everything else until the avid kissing was broken by a muffled curse and one of the hands holding her in perfect place lost its grip on her fevered flesh. A shrill barking blasted into her ears, opening them to the outer world again, jarring her mind into sharp recognition of where she was.

And with whom!

Sheer shock thumped her feet back on the ground again, her arms flying down from their stranglehold on Nic Moretti's neck. Cleo was barking her head off and tugging hard on the leash that was looped around Nic's wrist, her claws digging at the gravel on the driveway in ferocious determination to pull the two people apart and draw attention to herself again.

Saved by the dog, Serena thought dizzily. It was paramount she pull her wits together to deal with this terribly vulnerable situation. If Cleo hadn't come to the rescue, she and Nic could have been tearing each other's clothes off and coupling on the lawn. Or against her car.

Car!

Miraculously she still had the keys clutched in her hand. She swung around, pressing the remote control button to unlock the doors. Hearing the affirmative click, she aimed a brilliant smile at Nic who was still busy persuading Cleo to calm down and come to heel.

'Got to go,' she stated firmly.

'Go?' he repeated dazedly.

'Yes.' She reached for the driver's door handle and yanked it open. 'I guess that kiss was a thank you.'

'A thank you?' He looked incredulously at her.

'Very nice it was, too.'

'Nice?' It was a derisive bark of disbelief.

'Goodnight. And good luck with Cleo.'

She jumped into the driver's seat, slammed the door shut, gunned the engine and was off before he could stop her or say anything that would deny her dismissive reading of what had actually been a cataclysmic event for her. She only just remembered to put on the headlights as she was about to turn onto the public road.

There was still enough light to see by but twilight was fast turning to night. The clock on the dashboard said eight forty-five. How long had she been in that clinch with Nic Moretti, telling him she was his for the taking? She'd lost all her bearings, as though an earthquake had hit her. In fact, she was still trembling.

Having made her escape and travelled enough distance to feel safe, Serena pulled over to the verge of the road and cut the engine. Feeling in desperate need of liberal doses of oxygen to her fevered brain, she wound down her window and took several deep breaths of fresh cool air.

The awful truth was, the big bad wolf had pounced and she'd been only too eager to be gobbled up. No hiding that. But she didn't have to put herself at risk again.

The worst of it was, in all her twenty-eight years, no man had ever drawn such an overwhelming response from her. This had to be some diabolical trick of chemistry because it was very clear in Serena's mind that she didn't fit into Nic Moretti's world and never would.

He was a high-flyer. He'd marry one of his own kind. No way would he climb down enough to consider her a suitable mate for life. The only mating he'd want with her would be strictly on the side, and she was not going to put herself in that position.

Absolutely not!

A kiss was just a kiss, she told herself, as she restarted the car and headed for home.

But what a kiss!

CHAPTER SIX

NIC let the damned dog take *him* for a walk around the lawn. He was in a total daze, his mind shot through with disbelief. Serena Fleming was a challenging cutie but he hadn't expected her to blow him away. On two counts! First, punching him out with a powerhouse of passion, then kissing him off with a dismissive goodbye.

He shook his head.

This didn't happen to him.

In all his years of dating women, never had a first kiss spun him out of a controlled awareness of how it was going for both himself and the other participant. Completely losing it was incomprehensible to him, especially over a pert little chick with whom he had nothing in common apart from a problem with a dog.

No denying she raised his sexual instincts sky-high. He had one hell of an itch to get her into bed with him. And moving right down to animal level, *she* had been on heat to mate with him. But for Cleo's untimely intervention, it could well have ended in a highly primitive *fait accompli*. Would Serena Fleming have dusted him off her then and made the same fast getaway?

Every woman he'd ever known had lingered for more of whatever he gave them. Purring for it, more times than not. Yet here was a slip of a girl, kissing him with stunning passion, then leaving him as flat as a pricked balloon.

Anger stirred. He glared at the dog who was prancing along, blithely careless of the frustration it had caused. 'She cares more about you than she does about me.'

Cleo paused and looked at him with soulful eyes.

'You needn't think I'm taking *you* to bed with me,' Nic growled. 'You go into your cave tonight.'

He was feeling distinctly cavemanlike himself. In fact, if Serena Fleming was still here, he'd throw her over his shoulder, slap her provocative backside, and haul her off to a sexual orgy that would give him intense satisfaction and reduce her to his willing slave.

Which just went to prove how far she'd got under his skin.

Nic usually prided himself on being a highly civilised man, considerate of others, obliging their needs where they didn't clash too much with his own, caring about their sensitivities, playing the diplomat with finesse. Clearly there was some strange mutant chemistry at work here with the dog-handler, changing parameters he had always controlled.

The sensible course was to simply let her go, limit their encounters to the brief dog pick-ups and deliveries every Monday. No problem with that arrangement. It was foolish to let what was really an aberrational choice of bed partner get into his head like this, disturbing the general tenor of his life.

Having decided to sideline an obviously unsuitable attraction, Nic took Cleo inside and proceeded to lock up the house. He tried watching television for a while but ended up changing from one program to another, none of them holding his interest. Taking a book to bed with him seemed a better idea. He had the latest Patrick Kennedy novel to read—good author.

Having collected a king-size pillow and Cleo's trampoline bed, he led the little terrier to the mud room. Almost forgot the water dish. He moved that from the kitchen and placed it next to the doggy door, then followed all Serena's instructions to the letter. Half of him hoped her advice wouldn't work so he could take her down a peg or two, demand his money back, but he knew that was being churlish. Better that it did work so he could get a good night's sleep.

Amazingly, after a few initial barks to protest Nic's departure, Cleo did settle. Maybe the music got to her, or she decided the cave of blankets wasn't a bad place to be. Whatever... Nic wasn't about to check as long as peace reigned. He turned off all the lights and retired to his bed.

After several episodes of his mind wandering where he'd resolved it shouldn't go, he finally had the characters in the novel sorted out and was getting the hang of the story. Then the telephone rang, wrecking his concentration again.

He checked his watch since Cleo had his clock radio. Ten-thirty. He wasn't expecting a call from anyone at this hour. Was it Serena, ostensibly ringing to check the dog situation while surreptitiously checking his response to her? Maybe *she* was thinking about that kiss, suffering some after-effects, having a change of mind about leaving him flat.

Nic was smiling to himself as he picked up the receiver. This was his opportunity to be dismissive, which would put him back on top and in control where he liked to be. If Serena Fleming was hanging out for some pillow-talk, she would come up empty tonight.

'Nic here,' he said pleasantly, projecting perfectly good humour.

'Oh, Nic darling!' *His sister's voice!* 'You weren't asleep, were you? I'm calling from New York and it's morning here. Ward said the time difference was…'

'It's okay,' Nic broke in, trying not to sound vexed and deflated. 'I wasn't asleep. How's the trip so far?'

'I haven't managed a decent sleep yet. Last night I couldn't help worrying about Cleo. Is she missing us terribly?'

'She's fine during the day but she does miss you at night.'

'Poor baby!'

'In fact, I haven't managed a decent sleep, either, with her barking non-stop.'

'Oh, dear!'

'Not to worry, Angelina. I got some expert advice from your pet grooming lady and Cleo seems to have settled down tonight.'

'Michelle is quite marvellous, the way she…'

'It wasn't Michelle. Serena came and organised…'

'Serena? Who's Serena?'

'From the salon. Serena Fleming.'

'There's no Serena at the salon. Only Michelle and Tammy.'

Nic frowned at the certainty in his sister's voice. 'Well, she drove the salon van today, picking up Cleo and bringing her back, and she impressed me as knowing a lot about dog behaviour.'

'Mmm…Michelle must have taken on a new girl then. You say she's good? She's helped with my precious baby?'

'An absolute miracle worker,' Nic assured his sister while privately notching up a host of questions to be examined later. 'Cleo is now fast asleep in her own special cave of blankets with the radio playing classical music,' he explained to soothe Angelina's concern.

'Really?'

'Truly,' he affirmed.

'I know Michelle always plays music at the salon. She says it has a calming influence.'

'Apparently it works. Anyhow, don't fret about Cleo any more. She's eating well and we're getting along just fine.'

The little terrier had a very good appetite, as long as there was cooked chicken or steak or bacon on the menu. The tinned dog food was left untouched but Nic thought it wiser not to tell his sister that her precious pet had decided it would only eat what Nic was eating. Angelina would only fuss and what was the point? He could afford to feed the dog what it wanted.

He asked about New York and they chatted briefly of non-dog things. His sister sounded happy by the time the call ended, her concern over Cleo having abated.

Nic did not go back to reading his book.

He thought about Serena Fleming…about her quick wit and air of self-confidence…her ability to take charge…her disdainful attitude towards Justine who, on the surface of it, cut a stunning image that would intimidate most ordinary women…her experienced comment on the Chardonnay…and last, but not least, her incredible *sangfroid* in dismissing their clinch as a mere *thank you* from him.

Adding all this to the fact that she was very new to Michelle's Pet Grooming Salon, Nic was strongly reminded that his first impression of Serena Fleming was that he'd seen her before somewhere, most probably at some social function in Sydney. She might well have a city background. When he'd asked if she'd always lived in Holgate, her answer had suggested but not confirmed it was so.

The suspicion grew that she wasn't what she presented herself to be, but something very different and not ordinary at all.

The picture now emerging in his mind placed her as extraordinary, which made him feel considerably better about the whole situation. She posed far more of an intriguing challenge that he had initially assumed, and Nic knew he wouldn't rest content until he got to the bottom of Serena Fleming.

He grinned to himself.

In more senses than one!

CHAPTER SEVEN

MONDAY morning…back to the Gifford house to collect Cleo for her weekly grooming. Serena wished she could ask Michelle to do it, but that would give rise to searching questions and ultimately embarrassing answers. It would also be an unfair request since her sister's time was better spent in grooming the pets to the standard of perfection which was her trademark. In short, this was Serena's job and she couldn't shirk it.

Which meant facing Nic Moretti again.

He hadn't called about any problems with the dog. Presumably Michelle's instructions had worked and the nights were now smooth sailing. A pity she couldn't say that about her own. She'd spent many sleepless hours in her bed, going over and over what had happened with the testosterone loaded architect.

It was the sheer shock of her total vulnerability to what Nic Moretti could make her feel that had sent Serena skittering into her car. Fate had played a very unkind trick on her, placing such a bombshell in her path when she was fighting to attain some level-headed wisdom after her bitter disillusionment with Lyall.

Serena told herself it was just as well Nic Moretti hadn't attempted any follow-up to that devastating kiss because temptation was a terrible thing and it would have been very very difficult to handle, not to mention maintaining the dignity her self-respect demanded.

It took true grit to put herself in the van and drive to the Gifford house. Along the way, Serena decided she'd prefer a dog's life. Much simpler.

Michelle had told her about a silky terrier who'd flatly refused to be mated with her own kind. She preferred big dogs. She'd ended up with a litter by a labrador and a litter by a Doberman pinscher before her owners gave up on getting purebreds from her and had the terrier desexed. Only people wanted purebreds, Serena thought darkly. Animals followed their instincts.

No doubt Angelina Gifford would want Cleo mated suitably with another pedigreed silky terrier. Running wild would be frowned upon in that family, especially when it came to mating. A man might sow some wild oats but when it came to marriage, it was usually to their own kind. Only men like Lyall, who wanted an underling wife, went beyond the fold. And Serena knew what Nic Moretti thought of that!

She'd worked herself up into a finely edged temper by the time she arrived at the Gifford house. One bit of condescension or snobbery from Cleo's guardian and fur might fly. At least he couldn't think she'd dressed up for him. Her work clothes were the same as last week, though she'd teamed a plain blue singlet top with her denim shorts this morning so he couldn't possibly see a bare midriff as a come-on. And her hair was stuffed back into a practical plait. Not a skerrick of make-up, either.

Serena walked to the front door with stiff-backed pride and pressed her thumb to the bell-push rather longer than necessary. She didn't want to be kept waiting. Her feet felt as though they were on hot coals.

The door opened only seconds later. Nic Moretti filled the space with such overwhelming impact, Serena found herself retreating a step in sheer defence against the male dominance of his big strong physique, once again blaring at her since he only wore surfing shorts. Her hands clenched and the nails digging into her palms helped to ground her at an arm's length away from him.

He smiled. 'You're on time.'

He had a killer smile. Serena's pulse-beat soared. Fighting the dizziness in her brain, she poured out every word she could think of. 'I'm always on time. I consider punctuality a courtesy that I like to have returned.'

'Ah!' The smile turned lopsided. 'Black mark against me last week. I promise it won't happen again.'

The warm charm had the perverse effect of chilling her nipples. She could feel them tightening into hard buds, pushing against her sports bra. Any moment now he'd see them poking at her clingy singlet and he'd know...

'I take it Cleo has settled down at night,' she gabbled, desperate to keep his attention on her face.

'Your plan worked like a charm. I picked up a wooden crate to replace the bar stools. Want to see?'

'No, no, as long as it works. I must keep moving this morning.'

She tore her gaze from the twinkling invitation in his and looked down at the dog who was waiting at his feet. The leash attached to Cleo's collar ran up to a loop around Nic Moretti's wrist. Vividly recalling how treacherous that leash could be, Serena immediately crouched and picked up the little silky terrier, cradling her against her chest, which also helped to hide the aroused state of her breasts.

'If you'll just unhand the leash, I'll be off,' she said somewhat breathlessly.

He took his time unhitching himself from the looped strap, chatting on as he did so. 'My sister called from New York, wanting to know if Cleo was fretting for her. I told her about you helping me. The odd thing was…'

He paused and Serena made the mistake of meeting his eyes again, dark probing eyes that had the searing intent to scour her mind.

'…she told me there was no Serena Fleming working at Michelle's Pet Grooming Salon.'

Her heart kicked. Was he thinking of the seventy dollars he'd paid out for *her expertise?* But the advice had worked so how could he complain? She'd simply been standing in for Michelle whose knowledge was worth every cent of that money since it had produced a week of peaceful nights.

'She mentioned a Tammy,' he went on.

'Tammy's gone. I've stepped into her place,' Serena rushed out.

He cocked a quizzical eyebrow. 'New to the job then?'

'Not exactly new,' she quickly defended. 'I'm Michelle's sister. I'm well acquainted with the business she's been running for the past five years. And I have an affinity with animals, just as she does.'

'So you're helping out your sister.'

'More a case of helping each other. I wanted to get out of Sydney.' The words tripped out before she could bite them back.

'What did you do in Sydney, Serena?'

Danger…danger…danger…

If he connected her to Lyall Duncan now she'd die a million deaths. Not only that, she needed to cover her tracks on the animal front. Leaving herself open to an accusation of false pretences would not be good. Her mind zinged into overdrive, wildly seeking an escape with honour.

'I practised a lot of psychology.'

It wasn't a lie. Dealing with Ty's clients had been like conducting a therapy session more times than not. The salon policy demanded that everyone have a smile on their face when they left. One way or another, you had to make them feel good, happy if possible, at least better than when they had arrived. Of course, listening was the big thing. And the clients lay in curved couches when they were having their hair shampooed and conditioned, same kind of relaxation as they'd get in a psychiatrist's office.

'May I have the leash, please?' she quickly asked, seeing he was digesting this information at the speed of light and deciding a fast getaway was essential. Cleo was making no objection to being cuddled so shouldn't cause any delay.

Fortunately, Nic handed the looped strap to her as he commented, 'I thought you said you weren't a qualified psychologist.'

'I'm not,' she conceded, swinging towards the van. 'That doesn't stop me from using it to get the result

I'm aiming for. 'Bye now,' she tossed over her shoulder as she got her legs moving away from him.

He didn't pursue her, though she felt his gaze burning into her body, making her acutely conscious of being watched and examined from head to toe. It was a huge relief to put the van between them.

'Back at one o'clock?' he called as she opened the driver's door and leaned in, bundling Cleo onto the passenger seat.

She popped back out to say, 'Yes. One o'clock,' then climbed into her own seat and shut the door with too much force, revealing an anxiety to depart that she hoped he wouldn't pick up. Her fingers worked very fast attaching Cleo's safety harness and her own seat belt. She didn't exactly burn rubber driving off but her inner tension only began to ease when she was well on her way to Holgate.

Escape made good.

Except she had to face Nic Moretti again at one o'clock and she knew he hadn't yet wiped her off his slate. It was possible that the smile and the welcoming charm had been employed to put their association back on a friendly footing—more comfortable all around since they would be seeing each other every Monday. Also very diplomatic if he happened to need more help with the dog.

But the curiosity about her background…her life in Sydney…that demonstrated personal interest beyond what was required to promote congenial meetings. It smacked of wanting to get close to her, and *close* was very dangerous to Serena's peace of mind. Not that she had any around him anyway. The man had a sexual magnetism that had all her nerves going haywire.

She had managed to cut him off at the pass this time, but what about the next and the next and the next? Maybe she should just say she'd been a hairdresser and have done with it. Let him link her to Lyall Duncan. It would undoubtedly cool his interest.

She'd probably fuelled it with her reference to psychology. Stupid move! Though it had seemed brilliant at the time. Brilliant and satisfying, seeing the respectful assessment of her being recalculated in his eyes. Why knock that down? She deserved respect. Everybody did. There was nothing shameful about working in a service industry. Didn't he service people, too, creating architectural designs to please them? Just because he made more *money*…

Serena sighed away the ferment in her mind.

There was nothing she could do to change the status of wealth. And if Nic Moretti was such a snob, he deserved to be misled about her status. Not that she would actually lie, but he could mislead himself as much as he liked. It should be interesting to see what he came up with next!

Nic congratulated himself on the deductions he'd made about Serena Fleming. She had been in Sydney until very recently and grooming pets was not a job she usually did. It was her sister's business. More likely than not, Serena had held some kind of consultancy position where pushing the right buttons with people would serve her very well. And charging a whopping fee came naturally to her. Definitely a smart businesswoman who was not backward in coming forward.

Though that latter attitude did not apply to sex.

Nic wondered why. Surely she was the type of woman who went after what she wanted. Why back off last Monday night? Was it because she'd suddenly found herself not on top of everything, control completely lost?

He could empathise with that shock to the system. It hit hard.

On the other hand, he certainly wasn't averse to trying another dose of it, if only to see how far it went. Nic smiled to himself, pleased with the thought that Serena had been out for the count in their clinch, every bit as much as himself. But for Cleo...

Nic's smile broke into a grin as he realised Serena had been using Cleo as a shield just now. All he had to do was think of some ruse to get her guard down so they could meet on ground they might both find highly satisfying.

One o'clock.

Having made a point about punctuality Serena arrived on the dot. It was disconcerting to find the front door wide open. Should she call out or ring the bell? Was Nic Moretti home or was the house being burgled?

Cleo pranced straight into the foyer. Naturally the dog was confident of entering its own domain. The leash Serena held was pulled tight before she could decide what to do. Then the dog yapped and Nic Moretti strolled out of the kitchen.

Shock and relief triggered a sharp rush of words. 'You gave me a fright, leaving the door open.'

He paused, threw his hands out in apologetic appeal. 'Sorry. I'm just home from a business meeting and I knew you'd be here any minute.'

He looked incredibly handsome, dressed in classic grey trousers and a grey and white striped shirt. Serena's heart pitter-pattered in helpless array. She'd geared herself up to ignore his beefcake attributes, and here she was, faced with an even more impressive side of him, the polished businessman.

He gestured to the kitchen. 'I was making a pot of coffee. Do you have time to have a cup with me?'

Temptation roared through her. He was so terribly attractive and there was nothing threatening in his expression, nothing more than a friendly inquiry. 'Yes,' tripped straight off her tongue. 'That would be nice, thank you.'

No harm in being a bit friendly, she swiftly argued, stepping into the foyer, but closing the door behind her did raise her sense of vulnerability and she wondered if she was being hopelessly foolish.

Cleo tugged at the leash, barking to be freed. She unclipped it and the little terrier raced off to Nic who crouched down, grinning as he ruffled the silky hair. 'Want to be admired, do you? All prettied up with your pink bow?' He raised an amused gaze to Serena. 'Do the male dogs get a blue bow?'

She couldn't help smiling. 'Yes, they do. And they tug like mad to get it off.'

Nic laughed and straightened up, maintaining a relaxed air as he led into the kitchen and poured the freshly brewed coffee into mugs. 'Milk, cream, sugar?'

'No. Straight black.'

'Easily pleased.'

'More practical. I've had many friends who never have milk or sugar on hand.'

'Always dieting?'

'It's the curse of modern society that skinny is more desirable than a Rubenesque shape.'

'Not too skinny. Anorexic women are a tragedy,' he commented soberly, picking up the mugs. 'Let's sit on the terrace.'

'I can't stay long.'

'I won't hold you up.'

This assurance made it easy to follow him and she was enjoying the casual banter between them. They settled at a table overlooking the spa and pool. A sea breeze wafted through the sails that shaded them. Very pleasant, Serena thought. And seductive, caution whispered.

'Have you studied art?'

The question completely threw her, coming out of the blue. Was he digging into her background again? Playing some snob card?

It spurred Serena into full frontal attack mode, eyes flashing a direct challenge. 'Why ask me that?'

He shrugged, denying the question any importance. 'I was just struck by what you said earlier about a Rubenesque figure. Most people would have contrasted skinny with overweight. It showed you were familiar with the kind of women Rubens always painted.'

He was quick to pick up anything, Serena warned herself, but there was no harm in answering this. 'I did take art at school. I guess some of what I learnt stuck.'

'Do you ever go to exhibitions at the art gallery?'

A probe into her social activities? Where was this conversation leading? Although wary now, she decided there was no danger in this particular subject.

'When there's something special on,' she replied offhandedly. 'Like the Monet one recently.'

He had seen it, as well, and they chatted on about the artist's work—a really convivial conversation which Serena was reluctant to end. However she had no excuse to stay once she had finished her coffee, and while she had actually relaxed in his company for a while, there was no guarantee that would last long. Besides which, Michelle would be expecting her back at the salon.

'Thanks for the coffee,' she said, rising to her feet. 'I have to go now.'

He returned a rueful smile. 'Needs must. I'll see you out.'

He stood to accompany her and Serena was once more swamped by how big and tall he was. She was acutely conscious of him as he walked at her side through the house. He hadn't touched her at all—didn't now—yet the memory of everything she'd felt of him last Monday night was flooding through her, stirring her own sexuality into a treacherous yearning.

'Do you happen to be free on Saturday?'

The casual question instantly set her nerve ends twitching. Was this some kind of a trap? Had she just been lulled into enjoying his company, a paving of the way for another pounce?

'If you could join me here for lunch...' he went on, rolling out temptation again, on a much bigger scale.

'No, I can't,' Serena forced herself to say. 'My

niece is riding in a gymkhana on Saturday and I promised to go and watch her.'

'Well, a promise is a promise,' he accepted without any hint of acrimony. 'Where is the gymkhana being held?'

'At Matcham Pony Club.' Lucky it was the truth so she had facts at her fingertips to back up her reply to him.

'I might go and watch for a while myself. Take Cleo out for a run. Introduce her to the world of horses.'

Serena's heart started galloping so hard, it felt as though a whole herd of horses were trapped in her chest. She barely found wits enough to effect a graceful departure at the front door. Her mind kept pounding with one highly sizzling fact.

Nic Moretti had decided to chase her.

Chase her, corner her, bed her.

That was how it would go.

Somehow she had to stop this.

But did she want to? Did she *really* want to?

CHAPTER EIGHT

CUTTING up onions was not Serena's favourite job. Her eyes were watering non-stop by the time she'd finished. Despite washing her hands and eyes at the sink in the clubhouse, the pungent smell was still getting to her as she carried the platter out to the barbecue where Michelle's friend, Gavin Emory, was in charge of the sausage sizzle.

Blurred vision was to blame for the lack of any warning. Serena didn't even look at the customer waiting at the barbecue. What focus she had was trained on handing the platter of onions over to Gavin as fast as possible.

'Here we are!' Gavin said cheerfully, tipping the lot onto the hotplate. 'Won't take long to cook.'

'No hurry,' came the good-natured reply.

Serena's head instantly jerked towards the customer. No mistaking the timbre of *that voice*. Hearing it so unexpectedly was almost enough to cause a heart seizure.

Nic Moretti grinned at her. 'Hi! Beautiful day, isn't it?'

'You came!' The words shot out before she could catch them back, revealing she'd been on the lookout for him, missed him, given up on seeing him here at the gymkhana, and now that he had come, he shouldn't have because she'd settled in her mind that he wouldn't.

'Great spot for a picnic,' he enthused, ignoring her accusatory tone. 'Wonderful trees. Plenty of shade. Lush grass. I brought a rug with me. Thought I'd relax and watch the riders go through their paces.'

'Where is...?' She looked down and there was the silky terrier under the trestle table which held the buttered rolls, bread and condiments, chomping away on a cooked sausage, oblivious to anything but food.

'She didn't want to wait for onions,' Nic said offhandedly. 'Didn't want mustard or sauce, either. Cleo likes her meat straight.'

Serena took a deep breath and moved behind the trestle table, blinking rapidly to clear the stinging moisture from her eyes. Nic Moretti had brought the dog. He couldn't *corner* her here. Not seriously. Too much public interference. So she had nothing to worry about. The only problem was in fighting his attraction.

'What have you ordered?' she asked, trying not to notice the way he filled his red and white checked sports shirt and blue jeans.

'Two rolls with the lot,' he answered, his dazzling grin sabotaging Serena's attempt to remain cool and collected. 'I've just been chatting with your sister...'

Shock slammed into her heart. *What had he wormed out of Michelle?*

'Met your niece, too. Charming girl.'

Serena gritted her teeth. Charm was undoubtedly what he'd used to get what he wanted out of her family.

'They told me Erin would be riding in an event at two o'clock.' He checked his watch. 'One-fifteen now. Will you be finished up here by then?'

'Sure she will,' Gavin chimed in. 'My daughter's riding in the same event.'

'Ah! Double interest!' Nic pounced, his eyes twinkling a challenge at Serena. 'Will you join me then and explain the finer points of the event?'

If she didn't, he'd come looking for her again, imposing his presence anyway. 'Okay,' she agreed, thinking her best defence was to get a few things out in the open with Nic Moretti. In private.

He chatted on to Gavin about the pony club until the onions were cooked and he was served with the sausage rolls he'd ordered. The moment he was gone, Gavin turned to her with a knowing grin. 'Nice guy!'

'More a master of manipulation,' Serena muttered darkly. 'I've got to go and see Michelle. Can you manage on your own?'

'No problem.'

There were problems aplenty in Serena's mind as she hot-footed it to the pony yard beyond the amenities block, hoping to find her sister and niece there. She needed to know just how much they'd blabbed to Nic Moretti before she tackled him herself. Luckily they were both there, along with Gavin's daughter, Tamsin, who was Erin's best friend.

Serena briefly reflected on how very chummy the two families were, and since Gavin was a widower, maybe there was no reason to be concerned about her sister's single state continuing for much longer. Right now, however, she was more concerned about her own entanglement with Nic Moretti who was definitely pursuing a coupling.

Michelle spotted her approach and moved to meet her, leaving the two girls to look after their ponies.

'You'll never guess who came and introduced himself to us,' she said, eyes sparkling with speculation.

'Cleo's keeper,' Serena answered dryly.

'What a nice guy! As well as gorgeous!'

'Did he happen to ask about me?' Serena pressed, ignoring both accolades since the *gorgeous* part was only too evident and it suited Nic's purpose to be *nice*.

'Only where to find you.'

'No questions about my past?'

'None at all. He did say you'd been great with Cleo. Mostly he asked about the gymkhana and chatted to Erin about how long she'd been riding. No really personal stuff.'

No reason for it if his only quest was bed. Serena was ruminating on this—her mind torn between relief and disappointment—as her sister rattled on.

'Gavin has asked me to dinner at his place tonight. And Erin will want to sleep over with Tamsin. Any chance that Nic Moretti will ask you out?'

Serena frowned at her. 'What happened to the warning about the big bad wolf?'

Michelle grinned. 'He has great teeth.'

'All the better to bite me with.'

'Come on, Serena. You're attracted. He's attracted. Might be just the man to get you over Lyall Duncan.'

'They're two of a kind,' she flashed bitterly.

Michelle shook her head. 'He wasn't patronising to either me or Erin. Not like Lyall.'

'You didn't tell me that before. I thought you liked Lyall.'

'At the time you could see no wrong in him. I just

let it pass, hoping you'd wake up to what you were getting before you married him. And you did.'

Thanks to Nic Moretti!

'Anyhow, what you choose to do is your business, Serena. I was just letting you know Erin and I won't be home tonight. Okay?'

'You *liked* Nic?'

'Yes, I did.'

It didn't prove anything. Angelina Gifford's observation just seemed more pertinent—*There wasn't a female alive who didn't love Nic.*

Michelle reached out and squeezed her arm. 'You know, I've learnt it's wrong to judge everything from a hurt that someone else has inflicted. Sometimes it's good…just to follow your instincts.'

She was referring to her own life—how the tragedy of her husband's death had cast a long shadow on her thinking, making her ultra-cautious and reluctant to let people get close.

Serena leaned over and kissed her older sister's cheek. 'I'm glad Gavin came along. Must get back to the sausage sizzle now. I've left him managing on his own.'

For the rest of the afternoon, the conversation with Michelle kept popping into Serena's mind, even though she rejected it as not applicable to her situation with Nic Moretti. She *knew* he was a snob, even though she couldn't once accuse him of being patronising in either speech or manner while they watched the riding events together. To make matters worse, being with him stirred instincts that waged a continual war with her brain, because following *them* meant abandoning all the common sense she was trying to cling to. In fact, most of the time they prompted things she had no control over.

He smiled and her facial muscles instinctively responded.

His arm brushed hers and her skin tingled with excitement.

He spoke and her heart played hopscotch to the tune of his voice.

If his gaze met hers for more than a few seconds, her body temperature heated up.

All of which brought Serena to the conclusion that she was hopelessly in lust with the man—a totally physical thing that she couldn't squash, shake off, or block. And maybe—just maybe—she should let nature take its course, especially since she'd never been affected like this before. There was something to be said for experiencing the highs in life, even if they were followed by lows.

This mental seesaw came to an abrupt crisis point when Nic casually asked, 'Doing anything in particular after the gymkhana?'

'No,' slid off her tongue, completely wiping out any ready excuses for rejecting the imminent invitation.

'I've got some great T-bone steaks and a good bottle of red. How are you at throwing a salad together? We could do a barbecue out by the pool, have a swim...'

'Sounds good,' she heard herself say, a sense of sheer recklessness buzzing through her mind. 'I have a deft hand with lettuce leaves.'

He laughed and there was no mistaking the triumphant satisfaction dancing in his eyes.

Cornered!

But not bedded yet.

Let him make one snobbish remark—just one—Serena silently and fiercely resolved, and lust would go on ice so fast, *his* head would spin.

His mouth twitched into a quizzical little smile. 'Why do I get the feeling I've just been put on trial?'

'Probably because I have the feeling you take too much for granted,' she retorted, raising a challenging eyebrow.

'With you, that would definitely be a mistake,' he declared, but there was wicked mischief in his eyes. 'Should *I* make the salad?'

She laughed at the ridiculously trivial point. 'No. I'll bring it with me.'

He frowned. 'I have the makings at home. We could just take off from here…'

'It's been a long day. I need to clean up first. I'll drive to your place with my contribution.' *And with my car on hand for an easy getaway when I choose to leave.*

'An independent lady,' he drawled.

'I like to be on top of the game.'

His eyes glittered with the promise of competition for that spot even as he answered, 'I'm happy to go along with teamwork. So when will I see you? Five-thirty?'

'Six. Gives me time to be creative with the salad.' And stops him from thinking she was only too eager to get there.

'I shall look forward to a gourmet's delight.'

A sexual feast, he meant. Every nerve end in Serena's body was twitching with the same anticipation, but no way was she going to admit it. Or go for it unless she felt it was right.

'Well, I hope I don't disappoint you,' she said, taking secret satisfaction in the double entendre. 'If you'll excuse me, I'll head off now. Have to let Michelle know what I'm doing.'

'Fine! I'll gather up my rug and dog and see you later.'

Nic smiled to himself as he watched her stroll away from him. Mission achieved. He glanced at his watch. Just on four o'clock. In fishermen's terms, he'd been playing out the line for three hours and he now had the result he wanted. More or less. Serena Fleming was a very slippery fish. He had her in his net but she wasn't leaping into his frying pan.

And she was providing herself with an escape vehicle by bringing her own car.

Nic reasoned he'd have to be fast tonight.

Very fast.

Knock her right off the top of her game before she could mount defences and retreat.

Funny…he couldn't remember relishing a date as much as he relished this one. The trick was to bring it to the end he wanted, with Serena wanting the same end, admitting it, accepting it, and wild to have it.

Wild…

Weighing up his memory of the kiss they'd shared had eventually brought Nic to the decision that *civilised* didn't hold a candle to *wild*.

CHAPTER NINE

SHE'D clicked off.

What had he said wrong?

Done wrong?

From the moment she had arrived until just a few minutes ago, Nic knew he'd carried Serena with him. The connection had been exhilarating—eye contact, mind contact, everything but body contact. Was it because the meal was now over that she was withdrawing into herself, shutting him out, getting herself geared up to evade what had been simmering between them before it came to the boil?

She'd undoubtedly felt *safe* with a table separating them, *safe* out here on the patio eating *al fresco*. Nothing too intimate about the open air. And she'd kept the conversation away from herself, peppering him with questions about his career, his recent contracts, what he felt were his greatest architectural achievements, favourite designs. Her interest had seemed genuine, yet her attention had started slipping when he'd described the town house complex he'd done for Lyall Duncan.

Her gaze had dropped to the glass of wine by her emptied dinner plate. She had the stem of it between her fingers and thumb, turning it in slow circuits. Her face was completely still, expressionless, as though the slight swirl of the claret had her mesmerised. There was no awareness that he'd fallen silent.

He'd lost her.

The need to snatch her back from wherever she'd gone in her mind was paramount. He'd been a fool to keep talking about himself, despite her encouragement. Such a one-way track could too easily become boring. He leaned forward, a tense urgency pumping through him.

'Serena…?'

Her lashes flew up, vivid blue eyes jolted into refocusing on him. But the distance was still there. He instantly felt it—an invisible barrier that was very real nonetheless. He tried a smile, adding a quick whimsical question to grab her attention.

'Where are you?'

Her responding smile was slow, a touch wry. 'I was thinking of all the connections you must have made. Friends in high places. Big property investors like Lyall Duncan…'

'Lyall is more a business associate than a friend,' he cut in, wondering if she couldn't see herself fitting into *his* world. Which was absurd. She was clever enough to fit anywhere. If she wanted to. That, he suspected was the big thing with Serena, choosing what she *wanted*.

Her eyebrows lifted quizzically. 'You don't mix socially?'

He shrugged, sensing this was a loaded question but not grasping the logic behind it. 'Business lunches. The huge party he threw to officially launch the town house complex. Lyall tends to big-note everything he does. He enjoyed parading me as *his* architect that night. We're not really connected beyond the professional level.'

He could almost see an assessment clicking through her mind. Whether it had a positive or a negative outcome he had no idea. What he did know was that this was shifting ground and fast action was required.

'Let's clear these plates.' He pushed his chair back and stood up, cheerfully announcing, 'Time for dessert. Angelina left a selection of gourmet ice-creams in the freezer—macadamia nut and honey, Bailey's Irish Cream, death by chocolate...'

She smiled. 'Okay, I'm tempted.'

Tempted by more than chocolate, Nic hoped, relieved to have her on her feet and moving with him. He quickly picked the leftover steak bone off her plate and called Cleo to give her the special treat of two good bones to chew on, which would certainly keep the troublesome little terrier occupied and out of play for quite a while. She settled under the table with her version of doggy heaven, happily gnawing away while Nic and Serena collected what they'd used and headed inside to the kitchen.

Serena walked ahead of him, carrying the cutlery and salad bowl. Her long blond hair fell like a smooth silk curtain down her back, making his fingers itch to stroke it. No confining plait or clips tonight. She wore a highly sensuous petticoat dress that slid provocatively over her feminine curves with each sway of her hips. It was white with splashes of flowers on it, some filmy kind of fabric with an underslip. No need to wear a bra with it, Nic thought, and no trouble at all sliding off those shoestring straps. Her honey-tan skin gleamed enticingly.

All evening it had taken the utmost discipline not

to touch her. The bonds of restraint were now at breaking point. Every muscle in his body was taut, all wound up to make the move he had to make. She might decide against the ice-cream, might decide to skip out on him. Her thoughts were still a challenging mystery but he hadn't missed the sexual signals. She was vulnerable to him. He had to tap that vulnerability before her mind clamped down on it.

Serena set the salad bowl on the kitchen bench and dumped the cutlery in the sink. Her mind was in total ferment. Nic wasn't a friend of Lyall's. It didn't sound as if he shared the same attitudes. There'd been a lightly mocking tone in his voice when he'd spoken about Lyall big-noting himself.

She automatically turned on the tap to rinse the cutlery while reconsidering the humiliating conversation she'd overheard between the two men. Might it not have been surprise on Nic's part that Lyall's ego would allow him to choose a hairdresser as his wife? Had he simply been stringing Lyall along while the choice was explained to him, giving understanding as a pragmatic business tactic? Taking a critical attitude would not have been the diplomatic thing to do.

'You don't have to wash up,' Nic said over her shoulder. 'They go here.'

She turned to find him lowering the door of the dishwasher which was right beside her. He proceeded to stack the plates he'd brought in, his unbuttoned shirt flapping right open as he bent down. It was a casual Hawaiian shirt with parrots and hibiscus flowers on wildly tropical foliage, worn over royal blue surfing shorts, ready for the swim he'd offered but she'd decided not to take up since it would only provoke more temptation and she hadn't been sure where she was going with Nic Moretti.

Still wasn't sure…but she found her breath caught in her throat as she was faced with a wide expanse of bare muscular chest, a line of dark hair arrowing down to the waistband of his shorts, disappearing but heading straight for the apex of his powerhouse thighs.

'Special place for cutlery,' he pointed out. 'Put them in.'

She scooped them out of the sink and bent to place them properly, only to realise too late it caused her bodice to gape and Nic was right there looking at her, impossible to miss a bird's-eye view of her breasts. Heat instantly flooded her entire skin surface, raising a sensitivity that jerked her upright in a hopelessly graceless movement.

Nic closed the dishwasher door and suddenly he was standing very close to her, and despite the high-heeled sandals she wore, he seemed overwhelmingly big and tall, making her feel frail and fragile. She shrank back against the sink, her heart thumping so hard she could feel the throb of it in her temples.

Nic frowned, raising his hands in an open gesture that promised he was harmless as he protested her reaction. 'You can't be frightened of me, Serena.'

Her mind whirled, trying to find some reasonable response. How to explain that he generated a sexual force-field that she had no power to fight?

Nice guy, Gavin had said.

Echoed by Michelle—*Nice guy.*

And he hadn't been patronising. Not at all.

So why did she have to fight?

'You…it just surprised me, finding you so close,' she babbled, feeling hopelessly confused over what she should do, knowing only too well what her body was clamouring for, but was it right? *Was it right?*

'Not fear?' he asked, wanting confirmation.

His dark eyes were burning into hers. She had the weird sense they were tunneling into all her secret places, finding the truth of *their* response to him, never mind what words she spoke. Everything within her craved to *feel* this man, and denial suddenly seemed like a denial of life, of all that made life worth living. This mutual attraction had to be dictated by nature. How could it be wrong?

A hand lifted and touched her cheek. 'Serena…?'

What question was he asking? She couldn't think. His fingertips were softly stroking down her skin, making it tingle, and her entire body yearned to be similarly caressed by him. The memory of the kiss they'd shared ignited a chaotic surge of desire, a rampant need to know if the same wild passion could be aroused again. Her chest felt too tight, holding in too much. Her breathing quickened, trying to ease the pressure. Her mouth opened to suck in more air, or was it being pushed out?

Her mind couldn't cope with all this rushing inside her. She lost track of everything but his touch, sliding past her chin, down her throat, under her hair to the nape of her neck. He loomed closer, his eyes hypnotically fastened on hers, simmering with the intent to explore the same memory that was jamming her thought processes. An arm suddenly looped around her waist and clamped her body to the heat and strength of his. Her hair was tugged, tilting her face up. Then his mouth was on hers, his hot, hungry, marvellous mouth, explosively exciting, smashing past anticipation and delivering more sensation than her memory had retained.

Her hands instinctively sought to hold him, pushing under his opened shirt, revelling in gliding over his naked skin, feeling the taut muscles of his back, clutching him hard so that her breasts swelled onto the wide expanse of his chest, imprinting them on him in a wild urge to press an intense awareness of her own sexuality, of all that made her the woman *she* was.

The hand in her hair disentangled itself and moved to her shoulder, fingers hooking under her strap, pulling it down, dragging the top of her bodice with it. One breast freed, revelling in the stripping of the fabric barrier between her flesh and his, a mega-leap in sensitivity. Better still when he freed the other and shed his shirt. Wonderful to lift her arms out of the straps and throw her hands around his neck, running her fingers through the thick texture of his hair, able to press a far more intimate contact, exultantly satisfying.

He kissed her and kissed her, a passionate onslaught of kisses that drove her wild with wanting more of him. And it was there for her to have, his erection pressing into her stomach, wanting entry, seeking entry, as urgently desperate for it as she was.

Driven by a frenzy of desire she rubbed herself against the hard erotic roll of his highly charged sex, wishing she could hoist herself up to fit where she should, needing to engulf him, possess him, draw him deep inside her to where she ached to be filled, over and over again.

Then his hands were at her waist, thrusting her dress down over her hips, dragging her panties with it. 'Step out of them,' he gruffly commanded and they were whisked away from her as she blindly obeyed— blindly, recklessly, inhibitions totally abandoned. And it seemed to her in the same instant his shorts were gone, too, discarded in a swift tumult of action that rid them of all barriers to the ultimate intimacy.

He lifted her, propped her on the edge of the bench, moved between her legs, and finally, blissfully, he was there, sliding into the slick hot depths that had been waiting for him, tilting her back so he could reach further, and all her inner muscles clenched around him in ecstatic pleasure. Her legs instinctively locked around his hips, an act of utter exultation, and he kissed her, driving the overwhelming passion for this moment of union to an incredible level of sensation, total merging, making her feel they were flowing into each other and every cell in her body was melting from the sheer power of it.

He muttered something fierce under his breath as his mouth left hers, then in a harsh rasp close to her ear, 'Please say you're on the pill, Serena.'

'Yes,' spilled from her lips on a sigh of grateful relief. She hadn't thought...didn't want to think now...only to feel.

And the feeling was fantastic as he moved inside her, a series of fast surges that left her on one pinnacle of exquisite sensation after another. Even when he climaxed it left her afloat on a sea of sweet pleasure.

She didn't want to move. Doubted that she could anyway. Her arms and legs seemed drained of strength. But for his support she would have collapsed in a limp heap.

His chest was heaving. 'Shouldn't have happened here,' he muttered, his tone raw, savage. 'Madness...'

Serena was beyond comment.

'A kitchen bench, for God's sake!' he went on, sounding shocked, horrified. He swept her off it, strong arms holding her securely against him, carrying her...swift strides being taken. 'Sorry, sorry...' The anguished apology jerked out as he seemed intent on rushing her somewhere else. 'I'll make it up to you, I swear.'

Why did it matter? Serena thought in hazy confusion. Was he worried that it hadn't been good for her? Had he somehow missed her response? Her head was resting on his wonderfully broad shoulder, her hands loosely linked behind his neck. She sighed, not knowing what to say, loving his aggressive maleness, trusting him to look after the next step to wherever they were going together. It was like being swept along in a dream she didn't want to end, and the best part was he was real. All she was feeling with him was real.

He laid her on a bed, a soft doona on its surface beneath her, a soft pillow under her head, lovely sensual comfort. He stood looking down at her, shaking his head in a kind of awed wonderment as his gaze travelled slowly from the spill of her hair on the pillow to the languorous satisfaction written on her face, the tilt of her breasts, the curved spread of her hips, the moist apex of her thighs, the relaxed sprawl of her legs.

She didn't mind being so open to his view. She could look her fill of him, too, his magnificent physique, the immense power packed into his beautifully male anatomy. *The man,* she thought with a fatuous smile, and dizzily hoped he was seeing her, thinking of her as *the woman,* because none of this would ever make sense to her unless such special terms were applied to it.

'I'm not a rough, inconsiderate lover, Serena,' he assured her anxiously. 'Let me show you.'

Rough? He hadn't done anything she hadn't wanted. As for the kitchen bench...it had helped, not hurt. He hadn't hurt her one bit. Absolutely the contrary. She hadn't needed foreplay. But she was curious now about his thoughts. He seemed appalled at himself for having lost his sense of what he considered a suitable place for sex. Or was it about loss of control?

She liked the idea of Nic losing control with her. Somehow that made it even more right, whereas a step-by-step attempt at seduction would have felt wrong. Was that what he planned to do now, or was he intent on proving something to himself? It wasn't clear to her. Nothing much was...except how he made her feel.

He moved to the end of the bed, gently picked up one of her feet and started to unbuckle the ankle strap of her high-heeled sandal. Serena was amazed she was still wearing it—both of them. They'd completely dropped out of her consciousness. He stroked the shape of her ankle, the sole of her foot as he slipped the sandal off. Her toes curled as a zing of excitement

...elled up her leg, fanning the embers of sexual arousal.

He lifted her other foot, caressing it in the same way as he removed its sandal and Serena almost squirmed from the exquisite sensuality of his touch. He knelt between her legs, skimming her calves and her inner thighs with his fingertips, her flesh tingling, quivering as he parted the soft lips of her sex and bent his head to kiss her there, flooding her with such intense feeling, her whole body arched in convulsive need for him.

He moved his hand to the same place, stroking to answer her need as he lifted himself up and hovered over her. 'Cup your breasts for me, Serena. Hold them close,' he commanded huskily.

She did. His mouth closed over them, one at a time, drawing deeply on them, lashing the distended nipples with his tongue, and she found her fingers squeezing her breasts higher for him, revelling in the wild voluptuousness of the action while his fingers were stroking and circling the soft moist entry to the seething need within, preparing the way, building the anticipation to screaming point.

Which was reached.

'Come...now...now!' she shrieked, unable to hold on any longer.

And he did, surging up and plunging in, shooting her to an instant shattering climax, then taking her on a constant roll of orgasms that totally rewrote her experience of sexual pleasure. So consumed was she by what *he* could do for her, she lost all awareness of anything else. Her hands found their own paths of sensual delight, gliding over the taut muscles of his body, touching his face, his hair. Her feet slid down his thighs, savouring their incredible strength and stamina.

Sometimes he paused to kiss her and she surrendered her mouth to his with a blissful joy in the heightened intimacy. Most of the time she just closed her eyes and let the marvels of their inner world wash through her, focusing on every magic ripple of it. And the final burst of melding warmth lingered on long after Nic had moved to lie beside her, his arm clasping her so close her head rested over his heart, their bodies humming a sweet togetherness.

He stroked her hair, planted a slow, warm kiss on it, murmured, 'I hope I got it right for you this time.'

Amazing that he doubted himself in any way. 'You did the first time,' she answered truthfully.

The hand stroking her hair stilled. She could hear the frown in his voice as he queried, 'But I just…took you.'

She lifted herself up enough to smile her totally unclouded pleasure in him. 'I took you, too. Didn't you realise that, Nic?'

The V between his brows didn't clear. She reached up and gently smoothed it away, still smiling to erase any concern in his mind. 'I've loved every minute of having you.'

Taking him? Having him?

It blew Nic's mind. Serena was still on top of this game while he…he'd almost completely lost it back there in the kitchen, going for it full-on, already inside her before he'd even thought of contraception. All right for her. She'd known she was on the pill. No worries there to slow her down or give her heart a hell of a jolt. Then not saying a word when he'd brought her in here, letting him make love to her to see what that was like as opposed to the raw sex event...no wonder she looked so smugly satisfied.

She'd taken him!

While he... Nic pulled himself up on the wild flurry of thoughts. He'd got what he wanted, hadn't he? Serena was in bed with him, happy to be here. So why did he feel screwed up about it? He should be feeling great. He did. But he wasn't on top of what was going on here. It was like...she was drawing more from him than he was drawing from her. He'd never had this situation before. The need to feel secure with this woman was gnawing at him. Why it meant so much he didn't know but he had to reach into her somehow and make their connection firm.

He returned her smile. 'Well, that's good to hear, Serena. I didn't want you to feel...badly used.'

She laughed a little self-consciously. 'Not at all. It was truly a mutual thing.'

'Fine!'

A thump on the bed startled both of them. It was Cleo who proceeded to prance around them excitedly, wagging her tail, tongue hanging out, looking for a place to lick.

'Oh, no you don't!' Nic yelled, hastily disentangling himself from Serena as he silently cursed himself for leaving the bedroom door open.

The little terrier evaded his first grab. It was Serena who caught Cleo—predictably!—and lifted her down onto the floor, laughing as she patted the dog to calm the barks of protest.

'No third parties allowed in here,' she said, then turned twinkling eyes to Nic. 'I guess it's time for us to try that ice-cream.'

'Good idea!'

Giving him time to win more from the highly challenging Serena Fleming. He didn't understand how he'd got so far out of his depth with this woman...or was he already in too deep to change anything?

If he just went with the flow...

Why not?

Wasn't he winning, too?

CHAPTER TEN

NIC scooped up their clothes from the kitchen floor and laid them on the bar counter separating kitchen from living room, moving away from them to go to the freezer for the ice-cream.

'Not dressing?' Serena asked, unaccustomed to walking around completely naked in front of a man, though she liked watching him, his beautiful body in motion, the slight swagger in his carriage that denoted total confidence in himself, nude or otherwise.

He threw her a wicked grin. 'Why give ourselves the frustration of clothes getting in the way again?'

She blushed, realising he wanted her easily accessible, sexually accessible. Lust not sated yet. And in all honesty, was hers for him?

He cocked a quizzical eyebrow. 'You're shy?'

'No. Not exactly.' She wanted it to be more than lust. A total connection. Was that too unreasonable, given their different backgrounds and circumstances?

'You shouldn't be.' His gaze sparkled over her. 'You're beautiful, incredibly sexy, and I want the pleasure of looking at you.'

The compliments boosted her confidence. It was silly to feel self-conscious. She had a good figure. They had just been deeply intimate. There was no turning back from that. Nor did she want to. Wherever it led, she was going with it now, tugged by feelings she had never experienced before.

Yet as he turned away to open the freezer, her mind flashed back to their very first encounter, with Nic opening the front door in boxer shorts, obviously pulled on for a modicum of modesty—*over an erection*—then Justine strolling out from the bedroom wing in a skimpy wraparound, another modicum of modesty in front of a possible visitor. They had both been naked before the doorbell had rung. And now here *she* was...naked...with the same man...barely a fortnight later.

Had he said the same things to Justine?

Stop it! she fiercely berated herself. Jealousy was an ugly thing. Nic hadn't chased after the penthouse pet. He'd dropped Justine cold and gone all out to set up this situation. *She* was the woman he wanted to be with.

He lined up four tubs of ice-cream on the bench beside the freezer, then reached up to a cupboard for dishes. 'Spoons from the cutlery drawer, Serena,' he instructed, flashing her his dazzling smile as she brought them over. Her heart started pitter-pattering again.

'I'll give Cleo some of the chocolate,' he said, spooning ice-cream from that tub.

'Chocolate isn't good for dogs,' she automatically recited, having heard Michelle give that advice to clients.

'She loves it. And everyone deserves a treat now and then, even if it isn't good for them,' Nic blithely declared, setting the dish on the floor in front of Cleo who instantly showed approval of this particular *treat*.

'Now you...what would you like? A taste of everything?'

She laughed at the tempting twinkle in his eyes. 'Why not?'

'Why not indeed?'

He put scoops of each flavour into their two dishes and returned the tubs to the freezer. She was standing in front of the bench, about to pick up her dish and take it to wherever they were going to eat when he moved behind her and rested his hands on either side of the bench, encircling her in that space, grazing kisses across her shoulder.

Serena forgot the ice-cream, sucking in a quick breath as her heart battered her chest. The seductive heat of his mouth on her skin aroused a flood of sensitivity that paralysed any thought or action.

'What do you want to taste first?' he murmured, bringing her mind back into focus on the dishes in front of her.

'The…' She had to think hard to remember the selection. 'The macadamia and honey.'

'Uh-huh.' He was nudging her hair aside with his chin to kiss her neck. 'Go ahead. You can spoon some up to me, too.'

She did, and continued to do so at his insistence, even though she was hopelessly distracted with him moving closer, fitting himself to the cleft of her buttocks, stroking her thighs, spreading his hands across her stomach, gliding them up to cup her breasts, fanning her nipples with his thumbs. It was incredibly erotic, the cold creamy taste on her tongue, the hot excitement of his touch, spooning ice-cream up to both of their mouths while he orchestrated the intensely sensual friction of their bodies.

'Hmm…I think I like the strawberries and cream

best.' The words were softly blown into her ear, making it tingle with excitement, too.

'Not…not the chocolate?' It was wild, talking like this, pretending to ignore the slide of his erection, reaching up to the pit of her back.

'Or maybe the honey…' His hands left her breasts and moved down to the triangle of hair between her thighs. 'You're like honey, Serena. An endless store. And I want every bit of it.'

She couldn't answer. He was so good at caressing her, tantalisingly gentle yet knowing exactly what was most exciting. She wanted him, every bit of him, too. It was all she could think of.

'Lean over. Elbows on the bench.'

She didn't grasp what he meant to do. She just did as she was told on automatic pilot, unable to bear any halt to the intense waves of pleasure he was inciting. His arm encircled her hips, lifting her off her feet. The initial shock of the position he was taking was instantly obliterated by the deeper shock of penetration, fast and deep, explosively exciting.

He held her pinned to him as he pumped a fast, compulsive, almost violent possession, and somewhere in Serena rose waves of fierce, primitive satisfaction. Her feet curled around the back of his knees, giving her some purchase in the driving rhythm. He clutched her breasts, moving them to the beat within. It was wild…wild…and a wildly lustful exultation swept through her as she felt him come, spilling himself deep inside her in uncontrollable bursts, the aggression melting, shuddering to a halt, his breathing reduced to harsh gasps blowing through her hair.

'I lost it again,' he said in a tone of shell-shocked bewilderment. His hold on her shifted to bring her down onto her feet, once more standing with her back to him. 'Sexiest bottom in the whole damned world,' he added as though he needed some excuse to make sense of *losing* it. 'I think it's time we had a swim. Yes. A long, cool swim. Out to the pool.'

And Serena found herself being swept up and carried, but she didn't feel so limp and dazed this time. She felt exhilarated. Here was Nic, falling into the role of caveman on the loose, though he seemed to want to deny the more hot-headed—or hot-bodied—aspects of that role, and Serena had to admit she was revelling in not only being the object of his desire, but also the reason for his apparently much stronger than usual sexual impulses.

'Maybe we should stay out of the kitchen,' she suggested, unable to contain a smile. 'Kitchens can be very dangerous places.'

He frowned down at her happily teasing eyes. 'You're a provocative little package of dynamite, Serena Fleming.'

'So what should I call you? Nuclear fusion?' she tossed back.

'That's about right!' he said rather grimly.

'Actually it's incredibly marvellous.' She lifted her head, kissed his ear, and whispered, 'No one has ever made me feel…so much.'

It stopped him. He looked at her with burning eyes, searing away any glibness from that statement. 'Well, fair's fair,' he said with satisfaction. 'Can I take it you'll be staying the night? You're not going to hop in your car and leave me flat?'

She laughingly shook her head. 'How could I walk away from this?'

'A bit difficult when I've got your feet off the ground.'

'Do you make a habit of sweeping women up to get your own way with them?'

'No. But you're very slippery so I'm holding you fast. Only way to guarantee keeping you with me.'

'I *want* to be with you, Nic.'

'You're not going to make some excuse about having to go home to your sister and niece?'

'They're away for the night.'

'Aha! So you came here planning to seduce me.'

'I did not!'

He grinned, triumph dancing into his eyes. 'Got you then.'

It struck a bad note with Serena, bursting her bubble of joy. 'Is that what it's all about to you, Nic? Winning?'

He looked taken aback, as though she wasn't supposed to realise that. It chilled Serena into firing another arrow from the same bitter bow. 'Am I just another notch on your bedpost?'

'Another notch?' he repeated incredulously. 'There's never been a notch like you in my entire life. You can take that as gospel!'

Relief swept through her. He was so emphatic she believed him. Even more so when his eyes flashed dark resentment, as though she had totally wrecked his comfort zone by not conforming to any standard amongst the women he'd known.

Fair's fair, Serena thought elatedly.

*   *   *

He probably shouldn't have told her that, Nic thought, as he walked on across the patio. Gave her even more power over him. None of this was turning out how it was supposed to. He'd only meant to play an erotic game with the ice-cream, get her melting for him, give himself the satisfaction of knowing she was totally on heat before leading her out to the pool, wiping out any thought she might have had of dressing and going home. Instead of which...

He must be out of his mind. Still, it hadn't put her off him. Quite the contrary. And he didn't know what to think about that. Except he had achieved one end goal. She wanted to stay the night. Which meant he could put her down on her feet now. She wasn't about to run away.

On the other hand, he liked holding her like this. It gave him the sense of being in control, directing the action. He reached the edge of the pool before he thought to ask, 'You can swim?'

She laughed. 'Yes, I can. But please don't dump me in.'

'A mutual dive,' he promised, still not wanting to let her go. He wanted everything to be mutual tonight.

For Serena, it was another first. She'd never gone skinny-dipping by herself, let alone with a man. It was a fantastic sensation, feeling their naked bodies sliding together, the water engulfing them like warm silk. She kept thinking this would be a night to remember for the rest of her life.

Even when they started swimming side by side, there was a sense of intimate unison about it, the shared pleasure of watching each other, smiling, enjoying the intoxicating freedom of being together like this, no inhibitions. It was a perfect night, a cloudless sky full of stars, a full moon rising above the fronds of a palm tree, the air still warm and balmy from the hot summer day. Again Serena thought this was like a dream, too good to last, though she wanted it to…wanted it to last forever.

They kissed and played a teasing game of catch-if-you-can in the water. Nic hauled her out of the pool and wrapped her in one of the towels he'd laid out ready before she'd arrived, but they were both too aroused to dry themselves properly. The towels were dropped as desire erupted into urgent need. A nearby sun-lounger was quickly put to use, providing cushioned comfort as they merged and found more heights to climb.

It was all incredibly idyllic, lying cuddled together afterwards, looking up at the stars, Nic asking her what she wished for when they spotted a falling one.

'I'm completely content,' she answered without hesitation, feeling nothing could be better than this.

He laughed a happy laugh.

They put Cleo to bed in the mud room, leaving her with the radio playing music.

Showering with Nic was another sensual delight, leading to an even more intense exploration of their sexuality. Anything and everything seemed so perfectly right with him. Brilliantly right. So much so, Serena was tempted into thinking that they *did* suit each other. Perfectly. They *belonged* together, at least on some primal level that wasn't influenced by outside factors.

And it didn't change when she woke in the morning.

It just continued on.

They had a late breakfast on the patio—eggs, bacon, tomato and mushrooms which they'd cooked together. Nic had pulled on a pair of shorts and found a sarong for Serena to wear. The mood was happily casual, yet bubbling with an exhilarating sense of togetherness that sharpened their appetites for more and more sharing.

Serena thought fleetingly of calling Michelle to explain where she was but decided her sister wouldn't worry. Besides, she didn't want to introduce an outside note. It might jar on this very special time with Nic.

But an outside note did come.

And it jarred everything.

CHAPTER ELEVEN

SERENA and Nic were in the kitchen, cleaning up after breakfast. The Sunday newspapers had been delivered and they were about to take them down to poolside when the telephone on the bar counter rang. Nic picked up the receiver, answered 'Yes,' a couple of times, then passed the cordless instrument to Serena with a rueful little smile. 'Your sister...sounding anxious.'

She frowned as she took the phone. It wasn't like Michelle to break into what was essentially Serena's private business. Something had to be wrong at home. 'What's up?' she asked without preamble.

'Sorry to interrupt but we have a visitor here and he's not about to be turned away,' Michelle rattled out. 'Can we talk or is Nic still close by?'

He'd left her to the call, heading out to the patio, carrying the newspapers and his mug of coffee, probably expecting her sister's concern to be quickly soothed. 'We're okay,' she assured Michelle.

'It's Lyall Duncan, Serena.'

Lyall! Her night with Nic had driven her ex-fiancé completely out of her mind. It was a shock to realise that had actually happened, especially when linking them had previously affected many of her reactions and responses to Nic. Now...the memory of Lyall was like an unwelcome ghost at a feast, casting a shadow she desperately didn't want.

113

'He's driven up from Sydney this morning, arrived about ten minutes ago,' Michelle went on. 'And he's determined on seeing you. Says he'll wait all day if he has to.'

'Why?' It was more a cry of protest than a request for information.

'Perhaps it's a case of absence making the heart grow fonder.'

'Not for me it hasn't.'

'Lyall isn't about to accept that message from me, Serena. He's actually demanding to know where you are and I can't really pretend I have no idea. As it is, I've left him out on the verandah, cooling his heels while I'm on the phone, *trying* to contact you.'

Serena heaved a fretful sigh. What on earth did Lyall think he would achieve, just landing on Michelle's doorstep and throwing his weight around? Was he looking to effect a reconciliation, having given Serena six weeks to reconsider her position? Did he expect her to be grateful that he'd come to offer her a second chance?

'Serena…?'

'Sorry…I just can't believe this. What's over is over.'

'Then I suggest the sooner you tell him that, the better. And the most tactful place to do it is here, not there,' Michelle said pointedly.

Which meant leaving Nic and all they'd been sharing because Lyall's super-ego couldn't accept rejection from a woman he considered his whenever he felt like crooking his finger. After all, he was a top prize for such as Rene Fleming, and she would surely have come to her senses by now.

Anger and frustration boiled through her at being trapped into responding to a man she didn't want anymore, and being forced to part from a man she did. But this was not Michelle's problem and it was unfair to leave her with it.

'All right! I'll be home in half an hour. But please try to get Lyall to come back in an hour because I don't want him there waiting for me. Okay?'

'I'll do my best.'

'Thanks. Sorry for the hassle, Michelle.'

Even more of a hassle if Lyall saw her arriving home in last night's clothes without the make-up and grooming appropriate to them. That could instigate a very ugly scene, especially if he was expecting her to be regretting their break-up. No way would he have imagined her plunging into intimacy with someone else. And of all men, for that *someone else* to be Nic Moretti...

Serena took a long, deep, sobering breath as she returned the cordless telephone to its slot on the counter. The sense of having been on a wild roller-coaster ride with Nic hit her hard, now that it had to be brought to a halt.

She didn't know the heart of the man, yet last night...last night...the connection had been so strong, so overwhelming, surely it meant as much to him as it had to her. And this morning...it wasn't just some amazing sexual chemistry that made it feel right to be with him, was it?

Her heart fluttered with uncertainties as she moved across the living room to the door that stood open to the patio. How *did* Nic feel about her? He'd insisted she wasn't just another notch on his bedpost, but where did she fit in his thinking? Had he put her in any context at all?

He sat at the table where they'd breakfasted, looking totally relaxed, perusing the newspaper spread out in front of him. She paused in the doorway, acutely aware of the tug of attraction that made what she'd felt with Lyall seem hopelessly insignificant.

But discounting the sheer physical impact of him, was Nic so different to Lyall when it came to other aspects of his life? Did he simply want women to be there when he wanted them, while his work and how he performed in that arena remained his central focus?

She didn't know.

She didn't know nearly enough about him, nor how far her feelings could be trusted in these circumstances. In fact, the only certainty she did have in her mind was that she couldn't resume a relationship with Lyall Duncan.

Nic's concentration on a news story was broken by a prickling at the back of his neck. He turned his head quickly and caught Serena staring at him—motionless in the doorway and staring with an intensity that instantly twisted Nic's gut.

'What's wrong?' He pushed his chair back, instinctively rising to fight whatever was putting distance between them.

Her hand flew up in a halting gesture. 'Don't move. I have to go. Michelle needs me at home.'

'Why?'

She shook her head, shutting him out of her family business. 'Just a problem that has to be dealt with.'

'Can I help?'

'No.' Her mouth tilted in a wry grimace. 'Sorry about this. Can't be helped. I'll have to dress and get going.'

She was off, heading towards the bedroom wing before Nic could assimilate exactly what was happening here. One minute the flow between them had been brilliantly positive, then...total withdrawal! Not even a sharing of the problem that had caused it. With a nasty little frisson of shock, Nic realised he'd ceased to count in her mind. Serena had cut him off...point-blank.

The urge to go after her, imprint himself on her consciousness again, had him striding into the living room before he checked himself. This was not a reasonable reaction. If she had to go, she had to go. Why should she share some crisis at home with him? They weren't *close* in the sense of confiding personal problems.

Which brought him to the question of how close did he want to get?

He'd had a couple of quite serious relationships in his twenties. Both of them had eroded under the pressure of separate careers—different life-goals and values emerging as the shine of *being in love* had rubbed thin and *togetherness* had gradually ceased to exist. A few of his friends had married, but were now divorced. In fact, he could only think of his sister and Ward as an example of love holding steady, regardless of the bumps in life.

He knew he was getting more and more cynical about *love.* Those of his cousins who were married had done what he thought of as the Italian thing, making advantageous connections that added to the network of the Moretti business interests. Over the years, his parents had lined up several *choices* for him, but he'd always refused to consider a pragmatic marriage. It turned him off the whole idea of linking himself to any woman for life.

His mouth curled in distaste as he recalled Justine's attitude about sliding out of promises on the principle that what people didn't know, didn't hurt them. As far as Nic was concerned, trust and loyalty were big issues. So was family.

He frowned, realising his thoughts were drifting towards exploring a lot more with Serena than he'd originally anticipated. But what was going on in *her* mind?

It was okay for her to rush off to help her sister. He just didn't like her switching off from him, not when he was still so switched on to her, wanting more. She was one very elusive lady, had been from the start, and despite having managed to keep her with him overnight, Nic had the uneasy feeling he didn't have her locked into any future continuance.

What made her pull away from him?

She'd done it last night when he'd been talking about the people he associated with.

She'd been doing it again just now.

It didn't feel right to Nic. There shouldn't be any blocks, given the intimacy they'd shared. Whatever was causing these shifts in Serena had to be uncovered, pinned down. Having come this far with her, he was not about to lose the ground he'd won, nor give up on knowing all he wanted to know about this woman.

Footsteps coming down the corridor from the bed-room wing...

Play it cool, Nic cautioned himself. *Let her go for now and plan for tomorrow.*

Yet the moment he saw her, head down, shoulders slumped dejectedly, his heart felt as though it was being squeezed and the impulse to take on and dispose of whatever this divisive problem was, roared through his head. Her name flew off his tongue.

'Serena...'

She stopped in her tracks, shoulders squaring, head snapping up, her body stiffening in automatic rejection of any approach from him, yet the wild look in her eyes was one of intense vulnerability.

The aggression building up in Nic instantly abated. She didn't want to feel any form of entrapment with him. Force wouldn't achieve anything.

She began walking again. Faster. Making a beeline for the front door. 'Thank you for the dinner last night. And breakfast this morning,' she trotted out in a tight little voice. 'I'll pick up the salad bowl to-morrow when I come for Cleo.'

She was going.

'If there's anything I can do...' he offered again.

Heat whooshed into her cheeks. 'No. Please... I have to hurry.' She quickly averted her gaze from his, fastening it on the door as she took the steps up to the foyer. Her neck was now burning, too.

Why leave the salad bowl when it would only take a slight detour—past him—to get it? Was she remembering the two sexual connections in the kitchen? Evading any risk of tempting contact?

Her hand was on the doorknob.

'It's been a very special time with you, Serena,' he said quickly, wanting to hit some positive chord with her before she left.

She paused, looked back over her shoulder, though her lashes were at half-mast so he couldn't see what she was thinking. 'Thank you for that, Nic. I appreciate it,' she said huskily. 'It's been special for me, too.'

But it didn't stop her from going. The door was opened and a few seconds later it was closed behind her. Nic stared at it, wondering if there was something more effective he could have said or done that might have broken this unwelcome impasse.

The day ahead suddenly felt very empty.

Cleo trotted up to the door and barked at it, as though she, too, was protesting Serena's departure. 'She'll be back tomorrow,' Nic told the little terrier.

Yet he didn't feel confident about what tomorrow might bring where Serena was concerned. Which set off a strong determination to move directly into her territory and stake a claim on it.

CHAPTER TWELVE

To Serena's immense relief, Lyall's yellow Porsche was not in the parking area provided for the pet salon's clients. At least she had some time to prepare for their confrontation. Having brought her own car to a quick halt, she burst into the house at a run, not knowing what leeway Michelle had managed to negotiate. Her sister met her in the front hall, hands up in a calming gesture.

'No rush. You've got an hour and a half before he gets back.'

Serena deflated on the spot. 'Where's he gone?' she gasped.

'Apparently there's some beachfront property up for auction at Wamberal and he wanted to inspect it. Said to tell you he'll take you out to lunch when he returns.'

Serena shook her head. 'I don't want this, Michelle. I don't want Lyall. I don't want to be with him, talk to him, or…or anything else.'

Tears of helpless frustration welled into her eyes and Michelle quickly wrapped her in a sisterly hug. 'I'm sorry he's putting you through this, messing up what you've got going with Nic. Did he mind your leaving?'

'I…I don't think so. He offered…to help.'

'There you are then. Nice guy. Just make it clear to Lyall your relationship with him is over and put it all behind you. I'm here to back you up if need be. Okay?'

'Yes...sorry...guess I'm too tensed up about it.'

Michelle drew back and gave her a sympathetic smile as she stroked Serena's hair away from her face. 'Chin up, love. This, too, will pass. Go and have a long hot shower and you'll feel better able to face the fray.'

Serena nodded, took a deep breath, and headed for the bathroom, grateful for her sister's understanding and support. Michelle's words, *This, too, will pass,* made her realise she was letting herself get too over-wrought with this Lyall/Nic situation. It wasn't any-where near as bad as when Michelle's husband was killed, nor the earlier shock and grief they'd had to handle when their parents had died in a car crash.

She'd only been sixteen then.

Sixteen and forced to grow up fast, tackle life as best she could because it moved on, regardless of loss. Though it was never the same as before. There were holes that couldn't be filled no matter how hard she worked or how far she travelled or how hard she played. The sense of belonging she'd craved, and had continually looked for in everything she'd done these past twelve years had always evaded her.

She'd talked herself into believing she could make it happen with Lyall. With him she could have the family she dreamed of having and they would all be secure in a wonderful home of their own. Lyall could provide everything they'd need or want and she'd love him for it. Her life wouldn't feel empty anymore.

A pipe dream.

Which had come crashing down at the realisation

that the man she'd decided to marry wouldn't stand up for her if someone put her down. How could she ever feel any sense of belonging with a man whom she couldn't trust to speak of her with love and respect? The seductive prospect of marrying money had instantly lost every vestige of appeal.

There had to be love. Real love. On both sides for a lifetime marriage to work. Never again would she compromise on that principle. Emotional security was far more important than financial security.

Lyall had been a monumental mistake.

And Nic Moretti might be one, too.

There was no ignoring the fact that he belonged to the same social arena that Lyall occupied. She could very well be jumping out of the frying pan and into the fire by plunging into intimacy with Nic. Yet she didn't want to back off. After last night and this morning…it hurt to even think of backing off. Somehow she'd already connected too deeply with him. Though maybe her feelings were being too heavily influenced by the incredibly strong sexual attraction.

Whatever the level of her involvement with Nic, Serena found herself totally untouched by Lyall Duncan when he finally turned up at one o'clock, a half hour later than the time he'd stipulated. She suspected he'd deliberately delayed this meeting so she'd be waiting on him—his time being more important than hers.

Determined not to invite him into the house, she walked up to the parking area, noting as he stepped out of the Porsche that his appearance was a perfect illustration for casual designer wear—cream jeans with tan stitching, a tan vest over a collarless cream silk shirt, sleeves rolled up his forearms to show off his Rolex watch, and, of course, his tan hair was artfully streaked with creamy strands to make it seem naturally sunbleached.

His physique was much slighter than Nic's, more wiry. He wasn't tall, either, his height only just topping Serena's when she wore high heels. Nevertheless, he could exude a charm of manner that made his amiable face quite handsome, and he always—always—looked a million dollars.

Trappings did have their impact, Serena thought, rueing her own susceptibility to them in the past. How many times had she excused Lyall's arrogance, thinking he had a right to it, considering how successful all his entrepreneurial ventures had been in the property market? But that didn't include the right to view her as someone who should be subservient to him.

He frowned as he took in her unsophisticated appearance. Her shorts and tank top did not comprise a suitable outfit for accompanying him today, certainly not to the type of restaurant Lyall favoured. She wanted to emphasise with absolute finality how very *unsuitable* she was for him.

His mouth thinned into a grimace of impatience. 'I told your sister I'd be taking you out to lunch.'

'I told you our relationship was over, Lyall,' Serena countered. 'I'm not going anywhere with you today or any other day. You're wasting your time here.'

Another deeper frown. Faced with rigid opposition, he tempered his arrogance, trying a tone of firm authority. 'I wanted to talk to you about that. You misunderstood what was going on in the conversation you overheard, Rene.'

'I don't think so.'

'That guy was my architect. No one you're likely to meet again,' he stated, as though it excused the offence. Or warranted overlooking it.

At least this statement echoed Nic's—business associates, not personal friends—but it painted her current situation with black irony. 'That's not the point,' she argued. 'It was the revelation of what you expected from me as your wife.'

'That was only what I said to him, not what I really think.' Lyall made a dismissive gesture. 'He's one of the Morettis. Huge in the construction business and they've got connections that run through everything to do with building. I mean, we are talking about money you wouldn't believe. Billions, not just millions.'

'So?' It was a defiant stance, hiding the cramp that had hit her stomach at this sickening information.

'So he brought Justine Knox to the party. Her family made a fortune out of mining gold at Kalgoorlie. Her old man is known as Fort Knox, he's sitting on so much loot.'

The penthouse pet... No doubt Justine was well accustomed to penthouses and everything else money could provide, putting her on the same elevated plane as the Morettis—an appropriate coupling of two huge fortunes.

'And since you couldn't compete with me, you put me down. Is that it, Lyall?' Serena asked coldly, feeling the chill of hopelessness running down her spine. She was way out of her league with Nic, even more than she'd been with Lyall.

Her ex-fiancé finally realised he might have to offer

some appeasement. 'I'm sorry, Rene. You weren't meant to hear those things. It just got to me…Nic Moretti being amused that I'd choose to marry a hair-dresser.'

A bitter blow to his ego.

Far more important to him than anything else.

'Well, I guess you evened up the score by letting him think you'd lined up an obliging little slave-wife instead of having to pander to a gold-plated heiress.'

He grimaced at her interpretation but Serena knew in her bones it was true.

'I swear it was a one-off thing, Rene. It'll never happen again. I love the way you are. I love…'

'No!' she cut in quickly. 'Please don't go on, Lyall. I'm sorry if it's not over for you, but it is for me.'

'But we had it good. I can give you anything you want…'

'No, you can't. You kind of swept me off my feet, courting me as you did, making me feel special…'

'You *are* special!'

Serena took a deep breath and spilled out the truth. 'I don't love you, Lyall. I thought I did, but I don't. I've met someone else who's shown me that what we had wasn't real. Not for me. I'm sorry, but there it is.'

'Someone else!' he repeated as though she could not have delivered a worse insult.

No doubt it would be if she tagged Nic Moretti's name onto it, but Serena wasn't looking for more trouble. She just wanted out. Eventually she stone-walled long enough for Lyall to give up beating his head against unrelenting resistance.

It was not a pleasant parting but at least Serena was satisfied it was final this time.

This was, however, a hollow achievement, doing nothing to stop the depression that rolled in on her after Lyall had gone. He'd deepened all her doubts about getting involved with Nic Moretti, adding an edge of sharp pain to them now that she had succumbed to the temptation of following her instincts.

Trust them, Michelle had advised, but her sister didn't know what she knew. Michelle had never aspired to the high life, had no experience of how it worked. Her only contact with it had been Lyall, and Nic was different to Lyall.

One of the big differences, Serena reasoned, was that Lyall was a self-made millionaire and liked to show it off. The Moretti family wealth was clearly a given, no need for Nic to demonstrate it or flaunt it. He'd had it in his background all his life, something he took for granted, yet it had to influence his choices…life choices.

Construction…architecture…it was probably a natural path for him, an extension of the family business, and he certainly had the talent for it. He enjoyed the work, too, liked seeing his designs translated into solid reality. That had come through very strongly in their conversation over dinner last night. He was a natural achiever, and maybe that was where she came in.

Nic had wanted her in his bed.

Possibly her initial resistance had made the achievement of that goal even more desirable, striking on a need to win.

So he'd won.

What came next?

Serena inwardly fretted over this all afternoon. When the telephone rang just before six o'clock, Michelle and Erin were outside feeding the pony and filling its water-trough. Serena was in the kitchen preparing their evening meal and she took the call, expecting it to be for her sister or niece.

It stunned her when she heard Nic's voice asking, 'Everything okay there, Serena?'

'Oh…yes…' she bumbled out, dizzied by a sudden rush of blood to her head.

'Glad to hear it.'

Nice guy, nice guy, went whizzing through her mind, planting seeds of hope.

'I realised after you'd gone, I have a meeting with Gosford City Council scheduled tomorrow morning,' he went on. 'I'll bring Cleo to the salon on my way in. Save you a trip.'

She managed to get her voice working properly. 'Right! Thank you.'

'And return your salad bowl.'

She shouldn't have left it behind. She'd been in such a flutter… 'Sorry about that.'

'No problem. But I was wondering if it was possible to leave Cleo at the salon until my business with the council is done. Could be midafternoon before I can get away.'

'We can keep her here for you.'

'Great! I'll pick her up on my way home.'

'Do you know how to get here?'

'I looked up the address. Same road as the Matcham Pony Club.'

'Yes. So…we'll see you in the morning.'

'Nine o'clock sharp,' he said, and ended the call.

Serena's heart sank. It had been all business, nothing personal. Apart from the mention of the salad bowl, what had happened between them last night might not have been. Indeed, delivering the bowl back to her himself, and the arrangements he'd made for Cleo, kept her away from the Gifford house and any material reminder of the intimacy they had shared.

Was this the first step to establishing a distance which wouldn't be crossed again? Having won the jackpot, with bonus points, had Nic Moretti decided not to risk getting more deeply involved with a woman who was never going to be a suitable match for him?

A one-night stand could be brushed off.

An ongoing relationship might result in a nasty comeback further down the trail if any expectations were inadvertently raised. Men with big money could become targets of avaricious women who'd be only too happy to sell a juicy story on them.

Serena almost made herself sick with these fevered imaginings. She didn't confide them to Michelle because she knew they sounded neurotic, and probably were. If Lyall hadn't come today, stirring all those snobby issues up again, she'd probably be taking Nic's arrangements about tomorrow at face value.

By the time she went to bed, a resolution had firmed not to cross bridges until she came to them. Whatever Nic had decided about their relationship was beyond her control, and if there was still a choice for her to make about continuing their relationship, it was better made when she could assess his response to her in person.

Michelle had a valid point. There was a lot to be said for trusting one's instincts.

CHAPTER THIRTEEN

THE next morning Serena worked hard at maintaining a calm, natural manner as she went about her chores. She had just taken early delivery of a poodle at the salon and was seeing the client out of the reception lobby when a fabulous red Ferrari arrived in the parking area.

It was five minutes to nine.

Serena could hardly believe her eyes when Nic Moretti stepped out of it, followed by Cleo on her leash. He'd driven a four-wheel-drive Cherokee to the pony club on Saturday. She wasn't prepared for this in-your-face evidence of huge personal wealth, even though she knew it was in his background.

Many people could afford a Cherokee, but a Ferrari…it left a Porsche a long way in the shade, costing more than half a million Australian dollars she recollected from a motor show Lyall had taken her to. The famous Italian sports car shouted class, style and performance, and it emphatically underlined the social gap between Serena and Nic Moretti.

The fire was right in front of her now, blazing into her eyes, and it would have to be self-destructive perversity not to step back from it.

She saw Nic pluck the salad bowl from the jumpseat and forced her legs into action. She didn't want him bringing the bowl to the salon where it would be a constant reminder of her *weakness* for this man.

131

Better to meet him on the path and take the bowl to the house, putting it away, just as any further personal connection to Nic Moretti had to be put away. It was simply too foolish to entertain any hope at all that there could be any real place for her in his world.

He saw her coming and waited by his car, his smile and eyes radiating a warm pleasure in her that totally scattered Serena's wits again. Why did he have to be so attractive? Why, why, why? she silently railed, unable to stop her heart from racing and every nerve in her body buzzing in conflict with what common sense dictated.

'Hi!' he said, his eyes twinkling an invitation to resume the intimacy that had been so abruptly put on hold yesterday. He nodded to the departing car of the poodle owner. 'I see you're busy already.'

'Yes. What happened to the Cherokee?' she asked, wondering if he'd deliberately deceived her with it on Saturday, playing down the huge difference between them.

He shrugged. 'It belongs to Ward. He asked me to take it for a spin now and then. Stop the battery going flat.'

She gestured to the Ferrari. 'This is yours?'

'Yes.' He frowned, picking up on her guarded expression. 'I guess you haven't seen me driving it before.'

'No, I haven't.'

His gaze locked on hers with forceful purpose. 'It doesn't change anything, Serena. I'm still the same man you were with on Saturday.'

The challenge sent a quiver right through Serena

but she stood her ground, managing an ironic little smile. 'It does show I don't know you very well, Nic.'

'A situation I'll be only too happy to correct if you're free this evening.'

Her stomach cramped as his sexual magnetism came at her full-force. Her mind whirled with the knowledge that he wasn't finished with her. He wanted more. And so did she. *So did she.* Yet if she succumbed to this attraction again, got in deeper, it would be all the more painful when it did end, as it inevitably would.

'No, I can't,' she blurted out. 'Be free, I mean. I have family commitments here. Especially during the week. Michelle and Erin…' She paused for breath, shaking her head at the excuses pouring from her mouth when all she had to do was say *no* and stick to it.

'Fair enough,' Nic replied. 'Disappointing, but fair enough. Can I pass *my* family commitment to you here?' he went on, holding out Cleo's leash.

She took it, and the bowl he handed to her.

'Haven't got time to talk now,' he said with a rueful smile. 'I'll see you when I return this afternoon.'

She nodded, not trusting what might come out of her mouth if she spoke. He took off in his Ferrari— magnificent man, magnificent car—leaving Serena torn between the desire to take what she could of him and the certainty she'd be heading for miserable humiliation if she did.

A little Peugeot hatchback could never match a Ferrari. The two were worlds apart. The invitation to join him this evening had to be aimed at more sex and Serena fiercely told herself she'd done right to put him off. She hoped Nic had got the message that she was not a readily available bed partner.

The day was busy. At four o'clock, Nic still hadn't returned to collect Cleo and Serena took off in the van to return the Maltese terrier, Muffy, to her owner at Erina, an elderly lady whose arthritis made any activity difficult. Today she was in considerable pain with her hip and asked Serena to feed the dog for her as bending over hurt too much.

Serena didn't mind the delay. In fact, she made sure Muffy's owner had everything she needed within easy reach before she left. If she missed seeing Nic, so much the better. It saved her from the torment of facing him again.

Except she wasn't spared *anything*.

The red Ferrari was in the parking area when she returned home and Nic was leaning on the post and rail fence that enclosed the grazing paddock, watching Erin riding her pony around the makeshift jumps course. As Serena brought the van to a halt outside the salon, he turned to wave at her, a happy grin on his face.

She closed her eyes, wishing she was a million miles away. He hadn't given up. He wasn't letting her go. And this was all too hard. It wasn't fair, either. Couldn't he see it wasn't fair? A surge of angry rebellion against Fate and Nic Moretti's persistent pursuit of her demanded affirmative action. He had to be told in no uncertain terms they were going nowhere and he had to stop impinging on her personal life.

As this determination shot her out of the van, Nic swung around to walk towards her, a perfectly groomed Cleo on her leash trotting beside him, a pink ribbon around her neck, *and* a pink ribbon tied around a large cellophane cone which looked suspiciously like a sheaf of flowers resting in the crook of his arm.

Flowers…to lead her down his garden path!

No, no, no! She wasn't going to be bought, wasn't going to be seduced…

'Nice place you've got here,' Nic greeted her.

The comment hit very raw nerves. 'You mean this property is worth quite a bit in real estate terms,' she bit out, coming to a halt and folding her arms in belligerent self-containment.

He halted, too, cocking his head in a quizzical fashion. 'Actually I wasn't putting a dollar value on it. The grass is green, the old gum trees are marvellous, the cottage garden around this country style house is very pretty. I was simply thinking what a nice place this is.'

Which completely wrong-footed her, but Serena was not about to be moved from a full frontal attack on the wealth issue. 'Well, it's not mine. I have no equity in it at all. Nor in any other property. And it wasn't bought with family money. There is no family money. Our parents died when I was sixteen and the farm they'd owned was heavily mortgaged. We inherited nothing. What you see here was mostly bought with the compensation payout when Michelle's husband was killed in the line of duty.'

Her outburst succeeded in forcing Nic to pause for thought. He eyed her with an air of grave consideration, weighing her emotional agitation and her strongly negative body language. Whether what she'd said had shattered some pipe dream of his, Serena had no idea, but at least he couldn't argue against the truth of her situation, which meant he had to take stock of it and deal with it openly and honestly.

Finally, to her intense frustration, he said, 'I guess you're making some point here, Serena. Want to tell me what it is?'

Her arms flew out of their fold into a scissor movement of total exasperation. 'Don't tell me you can't work it out! Our backgrounds are chalk and cheese, Nic. You turn up here in a Ferrari. You have an apartment at Balmoral. You're a top of the tree architect. And the Moretti family is...'

'Always in my face,' he cut in with an ironic grimace. 'Makes me wonder sometimes if it's an absolute hindrance to what I want for myself.' His dark eyes mocked her argument. 'Being a Moretti is a two-edged sword, Serena. At least *you* know you're wanted for yourself, not for what your family can provide or the influence they can wield. You have no concept of how much that can taint.'

Somehow he'd completely shifted the ground on which she'd made her stand, turning it all around so that *he* was disadvantaged by the wealth issue, not *her*. Serena shook her head, hopelessly confused about where she should be heading with him now.

He sighed, his expression changing to one of wry appeal. 'You know, for once I'd really like it to be left out of the equation. Could you try that with me? I'll keep on driving the Cherokee if it helps.'

Serena was still desperately trying to sort herself out. She'd wound herself up, completely blinded by the negative side of his wealth for her, only to be suddenly shown there was another negative side for him. And maybe she was doing him a terrible injus-

tice, judging from a prejudice that Lyall had fed
to her.

'I'm sorry…' Her hands fretted at each other as she
struggled to get her head together. 'I guess I feel a
bit lost with you.'

'So why don't we take the time to find out more
about each other?'

More time with him…yes, that was what she
needed. All her instincts were clamouring for it.
Maybe she nodded. Before she could construct some
verbal agreement, he pursued the idea, offering another invitation.

'While I was at the council today I saw a poster
about a new exhibition at Gosford Art Gallery. It
opens Friday evening. We could take it in and go out
for dinner afterwards. I hear the restaurant right on
Brisbane Water, *Iguana Joe's,* is very good. I could
book us a table…if you're free that night.'

A proper date, she thought, not an easy drop into
bed at his sister's home. 'Yes. I'd like that,' she heard
herself say, all the fight having drained out of her,
leaving the still simmering desire to have what she
could of this man.

He smiled and stepped forward to present her with
the sheaf of flowers. 'I passed a rose farm on the way
here. Thought these might say more eloquently that I
want to be with you, Serena.'

The perfume flooded up from what had to be at
least two dozen roses, a random selection of many
varieties and colours. 'They're lovely. Thank you.'
She offered him an apologetic smile. 'I'll try not to
be so prickly in future.'

He laughed and wrapped an arm around her shoulders as they turned to go back to the parking area. Serena was instantly swamped with memories of how physically intimate they'd been and she knew it would happen again. There'd be no stopping it. But she no longer cared where it might lead or how it would end.

Nic Moretti had just become a part of her life she had to live, regardless of the consequences.

'Got her back, Cleo!' Nic grinned triumphantly at the little dog riding in the passenger seat of the Ferrari. 'A bit tricky there, but I turned it around and reeled her in.'

He was buzzing with exhilaration and wished he could put his foot down and feel the power of the car. Impossible on these local roads and he didn't really need the speed. He was riding a high, anyhow, having broken the barrier Serena had erected between them.

He laughed and shook his head at Cleo. 'Who'd have thought I'd ever come across a woman who was turned off by a Ferrari?'

Clearly the dog was perfectly content to ride in one. But then Angelina's precious darling was used to the best of everything, as was everyone attached to the Moretti family. Nic readily acknowledged he and Serena had very different backgrounds, but he wasn't about to let anything deter him from having more of a woman who was…unique in his experience.

Tantalising.

Intriguing.

Challenging.

He didn't even mind waiting until Friday for her. She was worth the wait. He liked the fact that she didn't kowtow to wealth, made choices that felt right to her, spoke her mind without regard to fear or favour. No artifice. He looked forward to viewing an art exhibition with her, sure she'd give him natural, honest opinions, not the pseudo-intellectual arty stuff he usually heard at fashionable gallery gatherings.

'I really like her, Cleo,' he confided to the little terrier, who returned an appropriate look of soulful understanding. Nic took a hand off the driving wheel to ruffle the silky hair behind the pointed ears. 'You like her, too, don't you?'

There was no yap of disagreement.

Remembering Cleo's hostility to Justine, Nic felt fully justified in declaring, 'Trust a dog to know the heart of a person. We're definitely on the right track with Serena Fleming.'

CHAPTER FOURTEEN

STRANGELY enough, over the next few days Nic didn't even feel sexually frustrated by the wait. He threw himself into work with a zest that seemed to bubble through everything he did. It was as if Serena had somehow rejuvenated him, given him a new lease on life. When Friday evening finally came and he was driving the Cherokee to Holgate, he felt almost lightheaded with happiness.

Serena must have been watching out for him to arrive. He'd no sooner stepped out of the Cherokee in the parking area adjacent to Michelle's salon, than he saw her stepping onto the path from the front verandah of the house. No waiting. She lived up to her own maxim of punctuality being a courtesy. Another first amongst the women he'd dated.

She looked beautiful, elegant, and incredibly sexy in a one shoulder cocktail dress that shimmered in shades of blue and hugged every feminine curve of her body. Her hair fell in a shiny swathe over her bare shoulder but was swept back with a silver slide on the other side. She wore strappy silver sandals and carried a small silver evening bag.

Nic just stood and watched her come to him, doing his utmost to control a rush of primitive instincts that might not serve him well in these circumstances. He sensed a tense wariness in her approach and knew he had only won more time with her. She was holding

140

back body and soul until a deeper trust was established.

Keep it light, Nic told himself. *Make it fun.* If she was giving him the benefit of some doubt, he had to blow away the doubt. Only then would she open up to him. He smiled, relishing this further challenge, and his heart seemed to dance when she smiled back. 'You look lovely,' he said, pouring out the warmth of his pleasure in her while trying to contain the heat of his desire.

'Thank you.'

It was a slightly stilted reply and Nic moved quickly to open the passenger door, fighting the temptation to touch her. As she stepped into the Cherokee, he caught a whiff of perfume, a musky scent that instantly stirred erotic thoughts. It was just as well the driving wheel would keep his hands occupied during their trip to Gosford.

'So what are we going to see?' she asked, once they were on the road.

'The main exhibition comprises twenty years of pop posters announcing concerts featuring the band, *Mental As Anything.*'

She gave a sharp little laugh.

He cocked a questioning eyebrow at her.

A wry look flashed back at him. 'I'm feeling just a touch of insanity myself.'

'Then you're in the right mood to view such art,' he countered with an encouraging smile, aware that she was twitchy and wanting her to relax with him. 'There's also an exhibition of nudes by local artists.'

She expelled a long sigh, then dryly remarked, 'I bet the nudes are all women.'

'Would you prefer men?'

'A mix would be more interesting. Of all the art work I saw when I was backpacking around Europe, the one that sticks in my mind most is the statue of David by Michelangelo.'

'That could be because it's displayed so spectacularly in the Tribuna of the Academy Gallery.'

'You've been to Florence?'

'I've been to Italy several times.'

'Oh! Of course.'

She dried up. Heat whooshing into her cheeks. Gaze averted. Bad mistake to remind her of his family, Nic thought furiously, and focused on drawing her out about her backpacking trip.

No family wealth behind her, he reflected, as she described her travels, scrimping on lodgings everywhere, endless walking to save money, yet the walking had given her an in-depth experience of each country and its culture that transcended the usual take by well-funded tourists.

She'd only been twenty-one when she'd gone, accompanied by a girlfriend her own age, brave adventurous spirits taking on the world. He admired her resourcefulness, her determination to see and learn all she could, and realised her self-assurance came from having achieved her goals, fitting in wherever she had to, talking her way into groups that protected her, getting where she wanted to go.

He thought of other women he knew who'd done the grand tour in luxurious style. Talking to them about it was like ticking off a list of *been there, seen that*. Serena gave him a different view. It was more grounded. More real. He enjoyed listening to her. Very much.

She was more relaxed with him by the time they arrived at the art gallery, a well-designed building that faced out onto a delightful Japanese garden. They collected glasses of complimentary wine, browsed on huge platters of fruit, cheese, dips and crackers, viewed the paintings of nudes, listened to the mayor's speech opening the main exhibition, then took in all the pop posters which gave a fascinating insight of the change in street design over the years.

There was quite a crowd moving through the display rooms. It seemed natural enough for Nic to take Serena's hand, holding her beside him as people milled around them. It amazed him how pleasurable it was, this least intimate of links, the warm brushing of her skin, the acute sense of physical contact that was agreeable to her. Not once did she try to pull away. They were having fun. It was good.

By the time they left the gallery Nic felt they were in harmony. It was only a short drive to *Iguana Joe's,* a waterfront restaurant and bar, splendidly sited between the ferry wharf and the sailing club. Serena happily commented on its architecture, asking if he thought it was inspired by the Sydney Opera House.

'Only insofar as the visual effect is of a boat sitting in the water. The sails of the roof are a different shape and the deep blue facia being shaped like a wave just beneath them, is a masterly touch.'

She pressed for his opinion on other buildings that had changed Sydney's skyline in recent years and this conversation continued until they were settled in the restaurant and given menus to peruse.

Without any hesitation, Serena ordered oysters, to be followed by the char-grilled swordfish with crab risotto and fig compote. She was perfectly at ease in this classy place, and with a classy menu. It raised the tantalising question of what she had done with her life in Sydney.

'How did you and your sister manage when your parents died, Serena?'

Here it comes, she thought, her heart fluttering against the rise of tension that dispelled the far more comfortable sense of floating along in an enjoyable stream of light-hearted fun. But there was no dodging the reality of her life and Serena didn't want to. This was the acid test. If Nic Moretti reacted negatively to her having been a hairdresser, it was best she know now.

She took a deep breath, fiercely telling herself there was no shame in being poor, in having to take what work one could get instead of being in a position where choices could be made. Nic's expression was sympathetic. She watched his eyes, expecting critical assessment to take over from sympathy. A judgment would be made and all her senses were on red alert, acutely aware that this judgment would direct where their relationship would go.

'Michelle and I had no idea how deeply in debt our parents were, the farm mortgaged to the hilt because of years of drought...'

'Where was the farm?'

'Near Mudgee. Dad ran sheep. He bred kelpies, too. Trained them as sheepdogs.' She shook her head, remembering the shock of all she had known in her childhood and teens suddenly ending. 'When everything was cleared, there was no money for us to continue our education. Michelle had been studying law at Sydney University. She dropped out and managed to get into the police force.'

'And you?'

'I had to leave school. Michelle took me to Sydney with her. The only job I could get was as an apprentice hairdresser.'

He frowned.

Serena lifted her chin in defiant pride. 'I was determined to be so good at it they wouldn't think of letting me go. It was a scary time for us, trying to set up a new life together and make ends meet.'

He nodded, the frown clearing, his eyes taking on an appreciative gleam. 'I bet you were the best apprentice hairdresser they ever had.'

'I topped my classes and won competitions for hairstyle and colour. This gave me the qualifications to move myself into a more highly paid position in a trendy city salon.'

'So you kept on in this field until you trekked off overseas?' he prompted, apparently finding this train of events acceptable.

'Yes. In the meantime Michelle had married David and given birth to Erin. They were a very happy family unit.' Not meaning to exclude her from it, Serena knew, yet she had felt like the onlooker, not really belonging. 'I felt free to take off and travel,' she went on, brushing aside the private feelings which could sound too much like envy.

'Your sister was happily settled with her husband and daughter,' Nic murmured, nodding his understanding.

'Yes. So I took myself off. Luckily I managed to get casual work at an upmarket London salon to supplement my savings.' She smiled at the whimsical irony of finding a job advantage in being a foreigner. 'The clients quite liked having *the Australian girl* doing their hair. They used to ask for me.'

'I'm sure you brightened their day,' Nic commented, his smile seeming to approve what she'd done.

'Whatever…it helped. The salon was happy to employ me in between my backpacking trips. I'd been based in London for almost two years when Michelle called me about David's death.'

'Killed in the line of duty, you said,' Nic recalled. 'What duty?'

Serena heaved a sigh to relieve the tightness in her chest before continuing. 'He was a policeman. He'd caught up with a stolen car and the driver had shot him. I flew home straight away, and the next few months were…very hard. Michelle needed me.'

'Another huge upheaval for her,' Nic murmured.

Another load of grief. But how to explain grief to anyone who hadn't experienced it—the vast emptiness of the hole left in one's life at the abrupt and absolute departure of people you've loved and depended upon to be there for you.

'Have you lost anyone close to you in your family, Nic?'

'No, I haven't. Even my grandparents are still alive.'

He'd never had the parameters of his world shaken, Serena thought, couldn't possibly understand the effect it had. He looked so strong, invincible, and maybe that was part of his irresistible attraction for her, the innate confidence that nothing could ever beat him. Did that come from the secure backing of great wealth or was it in his genes? All she really knew was how good it felt to be with him—when she didn't feel torn about their different stations in life.

A waiter arrived with the bottle of wine Nic had ordered. As they were served with it, Serena's gaze drifted out over the water which had turned grey with the twilight. Life had many greys, she decided, and she was treading a very grey area with Nic right now, an area that could turn black.

Nic hesitated over breaking Serena's pensive mood, even though the wine waiter had gone. The guy at the baby grand piano, providing mellow background music for the restaurant, had begun playing and singing *Memories* from Andrew Lloyd Webber's musical, *Cats*. Maybe Serena's memories were very poignant right now and Nic felt he had to respect them, give her time to come back to him.

He reflected on his own relatively smooth path to here and now. No real bumps. No big loads to carry. No huge adjustments to make. All in all, it could be said he'd had a fortunate life. It made him wonder how he would have handled the dark situations Serena and her sister had faced. Impossible to even imagine. He could only admire their strength in emerging from catastrophe and the love and loyalty that bonded them in an unselfish sacrificing of personal ambitions.

Michelle giving up law.

Serena, becoming a hairdresser.

Nic shook his head. A wicked waste of ability. Yet

what choice had they had, given their need to remain together. And who could blame them for that after the tragic loss of their parents?

The guy at the piano raised his voice to deliver the last line of the song—*A new day has begun.*

It must have impinged on Serena's consciousness because her gaze swung back to him, a sad mockery in her eyes. 'At least there was money this time. To begin a new day,' she said.

He nodded, realising she was referring to a compensation settlement for David's death.

'Michelle couldn't bear to stay in Sydney,' she went on. 'I think buying the place at Holgate, working with animals again, was a retreat to what we'd known as kids. To Michelle it was, and is, a safe place.'

'It looks as though she's done well with it,' Nic commented, sincerely impressed by her sister's achievement in establishing an independent business to support herself and her daughter.

'It's been good for her.'

'What about you, Serena?'

She shook her head, a wry little smile tilting her mouth. 'It wasn't good for me. Not then. To me, nothing felt safe. I had this urge to live as much as I could, go after the high life, have the best of everything, forget any planning for a future that might be taken away from me in a split second.'

'I can see how you'd feel that.' He smiled encouragingly. 'So you talked your way into a high-flying job.' This was where practising psychology had come in, Nic reasoned, anticipating her move into some public relations arena.

She laughed, but it wasn't a laugh of happy

achievement. It held a hint of derision, and her eyes were suddenly diamond hard, biting into him. 'Do you need that from me, Nic?' she demanded. 'Something respectably impressive?'

He was instantly aware that the whole atmosphere between them had changed. There was no longer any reaching out for understanding. This was hard-core challenge.

She sat back in her chair, establishing distance, and the air between them bristled with electric needles. The back of his neck felt pricked by them. Even the beating of his heart was suspended, anticipating attack. His mind screamed that the utmost caution was required here, and sweeping in behind this instinctive awareness was the conviction that he didn't care what she'd done. He wanted this woman. Losing her at this point was unacceptable.

He gestured an appeal. 'I'm sorry if I assumed something wrong. Please...I'd really like to know what you did next.'

Scarlet patches burned from her cheeks like twin battle flags. 'I went to what is probably the most fashionable hairdressing salon in Sydney. Have you heard of Ty Anders?'

'No.' He shook his head. 'The name means nothing to me.'

She shrugged off his ignorance. 'Ty is much in demand by socialites, models and movie stars because he can create individual images. My upmarket London experience particularly impressed him. He took me on, though he insisted I be called Rene, not Serena, which he considered downmarket. So I became Rene Fleming.'

She seemed to fling the name at him, as though it should strike some familiar chord, but it didn't. 'I'm not in this kind of fashion loop, Serena,' he offered apologetically, excusing himself by adding, 'I'm a man. When my hair gets too long, I go to a barber.'

'We had many wealthy male clients, believe me,' she said ironically, then paused, perhaps reflecting on his reply. 'The point is…I learnt how the wealthy lived and I spent every cent I earned on going to the *in* places, mixing with the *in* people, wearing designer clothes which I found could be snapped up relatively cheaply from secondhand boutiques where Ty's clients off-loaded stuff they'd only worn once or twice. I was a fun, fashionable person who knew all the hot gossip and all the right moves. Ty had taught me how to flatter, how to cajole, how to press the buttons that opened doors. You could say I was…a brilliant apprentice.'

Her words were laced with bitter cynicism. Being an adept social climber had not brought her joy. 'So what went wrong for you?' Nic asked quietly.

'Oh, I breezed along with all this for years, telling myself I was having a wow of a time, playing the game you beautiful people play, right up until it culminated in a proposal of marriage from a millionaire,' she tossed out flippantly. 'I even thought I was in love with him. I might actually have gone ahead and married him.'

Her alienation from this whole scene was reflected in her eyes…a bleak disillusionment that rejected every aspect of *the high life*.

'Something must have happened to change your mind,' he probed.

She stared at him, her expression flat, unreadable. Finally, she said, '*You* happened, Nic.'

'Me?' It didn't make sense to him. She'd left Sydney behind before they'd ever met.

'I overheard you talking to my erstwhile fiancé at a party.'

He shook his head, still not connecting anything together.

Her eyes mocked his forgetfulness. 'I was left with the very strong impression that you didn't think a *hairdresser* was good enough to be Lyall Duncan's wife. And his reply to you told me I'd been living in a fool's paradise.'

Shock rolled through him, wave after wave of it as recollections hit him; what he'd said to Lyall, what Lyall had said to him, the initial niggle that he'd seen Serena somewhere before, her none too subtle scorn aimed at both him and Justine, the possibly vengeful desire to score off him, her rejection of that first sexual impact, her resistance to any follow-up, the questioning about his association with Lyall...

A waiter arrived at the table with the plates of oysters they'd ordered. Nic was still speechless, totally rocked by the revelations that now coloured his relationship with Serena. She flashed the man a 'Thank you,' and they were left alone again.

With an air of careless disregard for his reaction to her disclosures, she picked up her fork, then flicked Nic a wildly reckless look. 'Bon appetit!'

His stomach cramped.

She jabbed the fork into an oyster.

Payback time, he thought.

And felt sick.

CHAPTER FIFTEEN

SERENA shoved each oyster into her mouth and gulped it down, glad she hadn't ordered something that would need chewing. Even so, it was amazing that her churning stomach didn't reject them. Her whole body was a mass of twanging nerves. She couldn't bear to look at Nic. The shock on his face only added to her torment.

The end, she thought, knowing he had expected her to have taken a different course—a more *intelligent* course—in this latter part of her life, and the bottom line was she now felt ashamed of the choices she had made, hated herself for having spent years pursuing some huge empty mirage that she'd been fooling herself with—the dress-ups, the sophisticated patter, the importance of knowing all the *right* places and things to do. No depth to any of it. No real meaning.

It hurt that she'd wasted so much time on what didn't count at all. She'd been bottling up the hurt, determinedly keeping a lid on it, but it was seeping out now, mingling with the hurt of being found wanting by this man who tugged on every fibre of her being.

She picked up her glass of wine, needing to wash down the lingering taste of oysters, and the bitter taste of loss. Nic had belatedly picked up his fork. She watched the shells on his plate being slowly emptied and sensed he was forcing himself to eat, to see this

evening with her through, hiding what he really
thought behind a polite facade, which was what polished people did…playing out the game until the
whistle was blown and they could go home with honour.

Rebellion stirred in Serena. She was sick of sophisticated pretence, sick of dishonesty, sick of any
kind of game-playing. She waited until Nic had consumed his last oyster, then burst into speech.

'I should thank you for instigating the conversation
you had with Lyall about me.'

'Thank me?' He looked at her with dazed eyes,
uncomprehending.

'It was a humiliating wake-up call to what I was
doing with my life, but at least it did make me realise
I had to get out of it and find something else.'

Conflicting emotions chased across his face—guilt,
anger, pride, shame—all finally coalescing into a
burning flash of accusation. 'How could a woman as
smart as you even *think* of marrying a pretentious
egomaniac like Lyall Duncan?'

It stung. It stung all the more because it portrayed
her as a gold-digger who hadn't cared to look past
the wealth dangled in front of her, and she had no
defence against it, except her own deep-seated need
to feel cossetted and secure, and the equally strong
need to ensure that the children she wanted to have
would always have solid support.

'That's over,' she grated out, shamed by his judgment though also resenting how quickly he'd made
it, not pausing to take her circumstances or feelings
into account. 'It's all over,' she went on, driven to try
to rebalance the scales in his mind. 'I broke my en-

gagement to Lyall. I resigned from my job with Ty
Anders. I walked away from all my *fashionable* connections. I was caught up in a stupid fantasy and I
woke up.'

He didn't take that into consideration, either. 'But
you didn't let it go, Serena,' he shot back at her.
'You've coupled me with Lyall.'

'How could I not? The two of you showed me
where I was in your very privileged world. Right on
the outer rim,' she argued. 'And you…your intimacy…with Justine Knox certainly reinforced my impression that social status was a higher recommen-
dation to you than any questions of character.'

'I'd made no agreement to *marry* Justine.'

Serena reined in the jealousy that had erupted from
her wounded heart. It served no good purpose. As far
as she knew, the woman was out of his life so her
argument was hopelessly out of line, anyway. She
was simply fighting the wretched feeling of being in
the wrong because she wasn't really, was she?

Not now.

The mistakes she'd made had been recognised and
she was intent on taking a different direction, had
already made strides towards doing so. She need not
have been so brutally honest about herself with Nic.
The desire to be done with false images had driven
her into opening up on everything.

The waiter returned to remove their plates, inquiring if everything was to their satisfaction. Nic's curt
reply put a swift end to his intrusion. The atmosphere
at the table was hardly conducive to genial chat.

Serena sipped some more wine, wanting to anaes-
thetise the pain. It didn't matter how much she drank.

If this was *the end* with Nic, a taxi could be called to take her home.

'You deceived me from day one, Serena. Deliberately deceived me,' he asserted, his low tone simmering with a violence of feeling which upset her even more.

'I did not!' The fierce denial leapt from her tongue. At least, she could defend this ground! 'You asked if you knew me and you most certainly did not know me. Which I told you.'

'But you knew me,' he countered.

'I didn't *know* you. I simply recognised you as the man who seemed amused that Lyall Duncan should choose to marry a mere hairdresser. Did you expect me to recall your part in a conversation that humiliated me?'

'There was no intention on my part to humiliate you,' he stated vehemently. 'I was just curious. Lyall Duncan is into status symbols in a big way. Marrying a hairdresser didn't fit.'

'Well, we both heard how it did fit, didn't we?'

'The man's a fool! And because I listened to his absurdly feudal idea of marriage, you set out to take me down, didn't you?'

'At the beginning...yes, I did,' she admitted. 'And I honestly felt justified by your initial attitude towards me.'

'What attitude?' he tersely demanded.

She flushed, wondering if she was guilty of misjudging again, yet there had been things that had made her feel...beneath his notice. 'The way you greeted me that first morning. I was so unimportant to you, a nobody whose name you instantly forgot, just someone you could use to alleviate an annoying problem. What I said and did was not so much to take you down, but to score a few points that made me feel better.'

'But once you realised I was strongly attracted...'

'You did all running, Nic.'

'And no doubt you revelled in that fact. Better still if you could bring me to my knees.'

That was so far wrong, Serena refused to dignify it with a reply. 'If you want to believe that, you go right ahead and believe it.'

'That's a cop-out, Serena.'

'For you, yes. Which is what you want, isn't it, now that you know everything about me. I'm sure you feel absolutely righteous about dismissing me as a nasty little schemer.' Riled by his wrong reading of her motives, she flung the snobby prejudice that had been eating at her right in his face. 'That certainly makes me *not good enough* for you.'

His mouth thinned into a grim line. His eyes and silence seethed with a violent challenge to her judgment of him. And maybe it was unfair, Serena thought despairingly. He'd never said it, never implied it, never acted that way. He'd given a reasonable explanation for the way he'd quizzed Lyall. It had nothing to do with *the person she was.*

With those intemperate words, she had given him just cause to believe she'd been playing some vengeful game with him. And in all honesty, she couldn't deny there had, indeed, been a payback element in letting the situation between them run on—a sense of having power over him.

She was so screwed up by *his* wealth and position,

and the fact that he'd been a party to that devastating conversation with Lyall, it was too difficult now to separate all that negative emotional baggage from the attraction Nic exerted. It was mixed up with things she'd wanted to leave behind, except Nic had linked her back to them.

In short, she was a mess again.

Whatever Nic Moretti was or wasn't, she didn't have the right to pass judgment on him or teach him any lessons. Her whole approach to him had been tainted by past events and she should have stayed clear of any personal involvement. Except…

'You weren't the only one who was strongly attracted,' she blurted out, shaking her head in sheer anguish of spirit.

Nic grimaced, shooting her a look of savage mockery. 'You've been neatly skirting around the truth ever since you met me. I don't even know if that's true.'

She heaved a ragged sigh, raising bleakly derisive eyes to his. 'Why do you think I'm here with you?'

'It's part of the pattern of your walking away, then making me work to get you back. That's a power play, Serena.'

A wry laugh gurgled from her throat. 'It's the power *you* have to override every bit of common sense that tells me to stop this…this hopeless relationship. I tried to lay that out to you on Monday.'

'My family has nothing to do with what I felt we could share,' he cut back impatiently.

'What? Some casual sex?' she snapped, completely losing all sense of perspective in the face of his continued assault on her character.

'There was nothing *casual* about it,' he asserted, looking fiercely affronted at the suggestion.

And he had every right to be because that wasn't fair comment, either. She knew the sex between them had been incredibly special, as deeply felt by him as by her. She was handling this badly, plunging straight down a destructive track and unable to pull herself off it. If there'd been any chance of reaching some understanding with Nic, it was long gone now.

'I'm sorry,' she said on a wave of sheer misery. Then in a last-ditch defence, she added, 'Do you think I enjoyed stripping my soul bare for you tonight? Did it sound like a power game to you, Nic?'

His face tightened. The blaze of anger in his eyes was averted, his gaze turned to the water beyond the open deck.

Black water.

Serena wished she could drown in it.

This, too, will pass, she recited with very little conviction. She gathered the shreds of some dignity together, pushed her chair back, and stood up. The action snapped his attention back to her.

'I'm sorry. I didn't set out to play false with you. Nor did I mean to inflict hurt. Things just…got out of hand between us,' she said in a tremulous rush, knowing she was on the verge of tears. 'I'm sorry about dinner, too, but…if you'll excuse me…'

There was no time for Nic to stop her. She was off, making a fast retreat through the restaurant to the reception desk and the exit. Frustration forced him to his feet. This conflict with Serena had not been settled to his satisfaction. She was right. It had got out of hand. Precisely where and how he wasn't sure, but be damned if it was going to be left like this.

He whipped out his wallet as he strode after her, extracting two hundred dollars and handing them to the startled receptionist as he passed her desk. 'To cover what we ordered,' he tossed at her in explanation.

He had no plan. His mind was in total ferment, stewing over everything that had been said and done between him and Serena. Adrenalin was charging his body with an aggressive drive to act first—catch and hold her—because nothing would ever be settled if she got away from him.

Through the glass doors of the foyer, he saw her half running, almost stumbling down the steps to the parking lot. She'd reached the shadow of the palm trees lining the driveway before he caught up with her and forcibly blocked any further attempt at escape by wrapping his arms around her.

'Oh, please…please…' She beat her hands against his chest. Tears were streaming down her cheeks. 'Can't you see this is no good?'

Her distress only served to convince Nic of the rightness in stopping this headlong flight away from him. 'It *was* good!' he fiercely insisted, the words pouring from feelings that would not be denied. 'Earlier tonight. Last Saturday and Sunday morning… It *was* good! And I won't believe anything different.'

Her resistance to his embrace crumpled, the fight draining out of her. She closed her eyes and shook her head dejectedly. 'You make me want to forget…what I should remember. There's too big a gap between us, Nic.'

'No, there isn't.' He gathered her closer, pressing her sagging head onto his shoulder, needing to feel the physical contact that had previously bonded them to a depth of intimacy he had never known before. 'Can you argue a gap now, Serena?'

The soft fullness of her breasts swelled against his chest as she dragged in a deep breath. The release of it in a long shuddering sigh was like a soft waft of her inner life seeping through his shirt and the words that came rawly from her throat opened the gates to understanding.

'I didn't want to want you.'

Pain…torment…

Like a thunderclap, it struck him that he'd delivered another kind of death to her with his careless conversation about a marriage that would have promised her every luxury money could provide. Not that he regretted for one moment that he'd been instrumental in breaking up her engagement to Lyall Duncan. She would have been wasted on a man whose ego demanded she worship the ground he walked on. But he himself had hurt her. Very badly. And unfairly. All on the spurious grounds that she was…a hairdresser.

She'd built herself a bright glittering bubble to banish the dark times and he'd burst it, stripping her of years of effort so she could step into a world he'd been born to. And what merit was there in a set of circumstances that gave him everything with no effort on his part?

None.

She was the one who had worked for it. And he'd unwittingly blighted it for her. Blighted it so comprehensively she'd walked away from all of it. What right did he have to blame her for being tempted to take him down a peg or two, or to show him she was a person to be reckoned with, not a walkover?

Her cry, *I didn't want to want you,* made absolute sense. His course was very clear now. He had to move Serena past that conflict, make her understand where he was coming from, convince her it was okay to want him because the wanting was very, very mutual.

He brushed his cheek over the silky softness of her hair, planted a kiss on it. 'You have nothing to be sorry for, Serena,' he assured her. 'I'm the one who should be apologising for my behaviour. That night at Lyall's party, I was bored. Bored out of my mind with all the big-noting that was going on. And I was niggled by Lyall's pretentious act of owning me. *His* architect. Not *the* architect.'

'It made him look good…you being who you are,' she muttered, a brittle edge to her voice.

'Not me. The Moretti name. He was riding on it. I expected his fiancée to have a name worth dropping, too, so I was surprised…and amused…when he conceded what you actually did for a living. I didn't even think of you as a person. I was irritated with Lyall and I needled him about his choice.'

'Choice!' Her head snapped up. Her whole body stiffened. 'You didn't even pause to find out what that choice entailed—the reputation I'd earned as a topline stylist. You just cast me as some kind of low-life…'

'Okay! I did do that. And I know ignorance is no excuse for what must have sounded like a snobbish criticism of you. I can only say it had to do with the person I knew Lyall to be, not the person he was marrying. And I'm sorry you overheard what was a mean and unkind act on my part. Sorry you were so hurt by it.'

She moved restively in his hold, still uneasy with his explanation. 'It was like…who I was inside didn't matter.'

'It does,' he pressed earnestly, knowing this was the core of her hurt. 'It matters more than anything else. And if I'd met you that night, Serena, those words would never have been spoken.'

She lifted her head and strained against his embrace, looking a pained protest at him when he didn't loosen his hold. 'It's not just me. It's an attitude. And being a victim of that attitude is not a place I want to go. Ever again.'

His gut twisted at the finality he sensed in those words. He had to fight it. He couldn't stomach losing.

'I swear to you it's not an attitude I live by,' he stated vehemently. 'On the whole I take people as I find them. And what I've found in you is what I want, Serena.'

He dropped his embrace to cup her face, to keep her gaze locked to his, desperate now to impart the intensity of his feeling for her. 'You've found something you want in me, too. Or we wouldn't be here now. And it was good. It can still be good. Even better for having all this out in the open.'

'No. It poisons things.'

'I won't let it. Trust me on this.'

'Trust?' Her expression of painful conviction wavered.

'Yes.' He dropped a promising kiss on her forehead. Then he took her hand, gripping it tightly as he pulled her towards the Cherokee, determined on drawing her into his territory and keeping her there.

'Where are you taking me?' It was a fearful cry. Her hand tugged against his.

He stopped to answer her, to use every persuasion he could think of, barely restraining the urge to sweep her off her feet and carry her away with him. Her face held the same wildly vulnerable look he'd seen on it last Sunday morning. It distracted him from his immediate purpose, the compelling need to understand everything about her taking instant priority.

'What was the problem Michelle called you about last Sunday?'

A flood of heat washed into her pale, strained face. 'It was Lyall. He'd come demanding to see me. He…he wanted…'

'To get you back.'

A nod.

'But you wouldn't have him.'

A shake of her head.

'Because of me?'

She took a deep breath, her eyes anxiously searching his, perhaps needing to know how much their connection had meant to him. 'I couldn't go back anyway. What I'd had with Lyall was gone,' she stated with stark simplicity.

'But against the whole tide of those past events, you did choose to stay with me, be with me, even though you didn't want to want me,' he argued, forcefully reminding her of how it had been. 'That says a lot, Serena. You can't want to cut off what we have together any more than I do.'

Helpless turmoil in her eyes.

'It's too good to give up,' he asserted strongly, and led off towards the Cherokee again, pulling her with him.

'It won't work! It can't work!' she wildly insisted. 'Let me go, Nic!'

'I can't undo the past, but be damned if I'll let it wreck the present or the future,' he declared with passionate fervour, ignoring her plea for release.

'But I'll be in the same place with you as I was with Lyall. Worse. *No one's* going to think *I'm* good enough for Nic Moretti.'

'Then I'll tell them why you are. And it sure as hell won't be in the same terms Lyall Duncan used,' he retorted fiercely, whipping out the car keys and pressing the remote control button to unlock the doors.

Before Serena could protest again, he had the passenger door open and took intense satisfaction in picking her up bodily and placing her on the seat where she'd be right beside him on the journey he was determined on their taking together.

'I shouldn't be letting you do this,' she agonised as he fastened the seat belt around her.

'When the going gets rough, the tough get going,' he recited, and stroked her lightly on the cheek. 'You're tough, Serena. You're like that mythical bird, the phoenix. You keep rising from the ashes. Nothing can put you down for long. And I refuse to accept that you'd be happy if you wimped out on us.'

He closed the door on any further argument, strode around the bonnet to the driver's side and climbed into his seat, closing his own door with a sense of triumphant achievement.

'I do have the right to choose,' she threw at him in one last challenge.

He returned a challenge of his own. 'Then make a choice I can respect, Serena. Give us a chance.'

CHAPTER SIXTEEN

THE warm tingling glide of fingertips trailing down the curve of her waist and hip drew Serena out of sleep and put a smile on her lips as she rolled onto her back and opened her eyes.

Nic was propped up on one elbow, a happy glow in his eyes. 'Good morning,' he said with a smile that transmitted he couldn't imagine a better one.

'Hi to you, too,' she replied, loving his unshakable confidence in the rightness of their being together like this.

If it was just the two of them in a world of their own, Serena knew she would have no problem with it, either. Last night Nic had been intent on carrying all before him and she'd been persuaded to let their relationship run on, to *give it a chance.*

It was impossible to regret that decision now. He was a fantastic lover. While sex wasn't the answer to everything, Serena knew she'd passed the point where she might have brought herself to give up this wonderful intimacy with him. Nic was right. It was too good to let go.

'*A new day has begun,*' he sang, then laughed and leaned over to kiss her. 'Our day, Serena,' he murmured against her lips. 'Call Michelle and tell her you're spending it with me.'

'You're getting to be a bossy-boots, Nic Moretti.'

'Oh, I'm sure you'll pull me back into line, Ms. Fleming.'

She wound her arms around his neck and shuffled her body closer to his. 'What about this line?' she teased, loving the feel of him, the scent of him, the taste of him. He was so beautiful, and sexy, and... Serena gave up on thinking as she once again revelled in the sensations Nic aroused.

Much later they let Cleo out of the mud room, Serena called Michelle to let her sister know she wouldn't be coming home today, and Nic set about cooking breakfast. He really was quite domesticated, Serena thought appreciatively, liking that in a man.

It recalled what he'd told her about his family last night. His father was a dyed in the wool empire builder outside his home—a bull of a man—but inside it, his mother ruled the roost, her husband indulging her every wish like a lamb, even to cooking Italian feasts for the family.

She fancied Nic was in the same mould as his father. He certainly had the strength of mind to pursue whatever his heart was set on. She wondered what it might be like to be his wife, then clamped down on that train of thought, wary of wanting too much from him.

She fed Cleo the meaty ring biscuits she liked, making a game of it by tossing each ring on the floor for her to chase and pounce on before chewing it up. Nic laughed at the little terrier's antics, commenting that he'd never thought of making a game of the breakfast food like that.

'You've taught me a lot, Serena,' he warmly added.

'Me?' She gave him a look of quizzical surprise.

He nodded. 'Forced me into reassessing quite a bit of my life. You're the best thing that's happened to me in a long time.'

She flushed with pleasure. 'That's really nice of you to say.'

'It's the truth.'

Nice guy…nice guy… Michelle was right. Serena resolved to keep trusting her instincts with Nic and shut out all the doubts that could spoil her pleasure in him.

He grinned at her, his eyes dancing with wicked mischief. 'You look very fetching in that sarong.'

He'd given her one from a pile kept for the Giffords' house guests. He was wearing nothing but a pair of shorts and she deliberately ran her gaze over his magnificent physique as she replied, 'Best we keep some distance. You're cooking.'

'Mmm…I do have a couple of burning memories.'

They laughed and bantered on over breakfast which they ate at the table on the patio. It was a brilliant summer day. It was easy to relax and browse through the *Saturday Morning Herald,* swapping comments on what they read. Serena pointed out a photo of a model on the social pages.

'I used to do her hair. Whoever's taken over from me is on a personal art trip,' she said in disgust. 'That style doesn't suit her at all.'

'You're right,' Nic agreed, then looked at her seriously. 'Are you sure that walking away from it is right for you, Serena?'

'No question,' she answered without hesitation. 'You've got to be full of hype to keep riding that scene and I'm done with pandering to people, day in, day out.'

'Do you have some other direction planned?'

'Not exactly. I thought I'd do some courses at the local TAFE college while helping out Michelle. Get myself some other qualifications that could help me move forward.'

'There's no particular ambition burning in you?'

'Not at the moment. No.'

'No dream career you want to pursue?'

She shrugged. 'I know it's unfashionable to have this attitude these days, but work has only ever been a means to an end for me. What I want most...'

'Yes?'

She grimaced, realising he could read too much into her dearest dream.

'Please...' he urged, sharp interest in his eyes. 'I'd like to know.'

'Well, don't take this personally,' she warned, frowning at the possibility that he might. 'What I want most is to be...a mother. And have a whole houseful of kids. Somewhere in my future.'

He gave her a wry smile. 'I guess that played a big part in why you agreed to marry Lyall Duncan.'

She returned a rueful look. 'It would have been a bad mistake. A marriage should be about loving each other.'

'That it should,' Nic agreed. He dispelled the awkward moment by going on to tell her about his sister's marriage, how Angelina and Ward couldn't have children but they were still very happy making a life together. 'And Cleo, of course, makes three a delight for them, not a nuisance,' he finished, making Serena laugh again.

They moved down to the pool and were enjoying a lazy and highly sensual swim together when they heard a car zoom up the driveway on the other side of the house. The alien sound intruded harshly on their private intimacy, triggering a nervous flutter in Serena's heart. Up until this moment, Nic had seemed totally absorbed in her, giving her a growing confidence in the relationship being forged. Now he was distracted, his mind dragged elsewhere.

'Are you expecting someone?' she asked anxiously, not wanting what they had been sharing broken by anyone.

'No.' He frowned. 'Guess I'd better go and see who it is.'

Both of them were naked. Serena had loved the physical awareness, the casual caresses that kept excitement simmering, the wonderful sense of being there for each other, freely within reach, no barriers. However, as Nic heaved himself out of the pool and fastened a towel around his waist, the security she'd felt in his company started slipping.

Cleo was racing inside, barking to let them know someone was at the front door, someone who might find her presence highly questionable.

'I'll send them away,' Nic growled, obviously vexed by the situation.

Serena watched him stride across the patio, wondering if he was vexed at the unwelcome interruption or vexed at the thought of being trapped into introducing her to someone he couldn't turn away—a close friend, an important business associate—someone who might find his involvement with a local nobody...*amusing*.

Goaded by this spine-chilling possibility, Serena scrambled out of the pool and raced to the sunlounger where they'd dropped beach towels. She quickly dried herself, fastened the sarong above her breasts, then wrung the wetness from her wet hair before raking it back behind her ears, effecting a reasonably tidy appearance. Just in time!

'Well, well, well, who do we have here?' a voice drawled from behind her.

Nerves screaming, heart clamouring, Serena spun to find a woman, having apparently chosen to stroll around the house rather than wait for the front doorbell to be answered.

And not just any woman!

It was Justine Knox, in full battle make-up and full battle dress, looking as though she'd top the polls at a photo shoot during Fashion Week.

The message was instantly loud and clear.

Justine had come for Nic Moretti and she still considered him *her man!*

But he wasn't, Serena fiercely told herself, quelling the sickening rise of panic. Nic had asked her to trust him. He wouldn't let anyone put her down. Not in his company. She had to give him the chance to prove what he'd said and this was undoubtedly a prime opportunity.

Justine came to a halt beside the spa where she had a commanding view of anyone emerging from the house, as well as the lower pool level where Serena had remained, determinedly standing her ground and refusing to feel intimidated.

On the surface, Justine looked all class. She had a wonderful mane of long tawny hair, falling in rippling waves around her shoulders. Her face would turn heads anywhere, strikingly beautiful. She wore a green silk top with a low cowl neckline above slacks in the same colour, printed with huge pink and gold flowers in an artful splendour that shouted designer wear, probably *Escada*. Gold chains adorned her long graceful neck, gold sandals on her feet, and a pocket-size gold handbag hung from her shoulder.

She looked stunning, and made Serena acutely conscious of her wet straggling hair, bare face, bare everything but for the sarong. On top of that, Justine was tall, statuesque, a much better match in physique to Nic. And, in other people's eyes, a more appropriate match in every way, Serena thought, her heart quailing again at the stark contrast between herself and the other woman.

Justine cocked her head consideringly. 'Do I know you? Your face looks familar but…'

Serena dragged air out of suddenly tight lungs and forced herself to reply, 'We haven't been introduced.'

'I'm Justine Knox, a friend of Nic's,' came the confident announcement, not the slightest hint of uncertainty that she might not be welcomed by him.

'Serena Fleming.' With a sense of doom rushing at her, she added, 'You were here when I picked up Cleo one Monday morning.'

'Good God!' Justine rolled her eyes as memory clicked in. 'The dog-handler!' Her perfect mouth tilted into a smirk. 'So that's why you're here. Nic's had more problems with the wretched little beast.'

Hot angry blood flared into Serena's face at the

patronising assumption. Before she could correct it, Cleo came hurtling out of the house, barking like a maniac at sight of Justine, who drew herself up in haughty contempt at the little terrier's fierce reaction to her presence.

Good dog! Serena silently but heartily approved. At least Cleo wasn't blinded by surface class. She recognised an enemy straight-off. Superficial glamour meant nothing to her.

Nic followed, looking grim-faced, his gaze cutting from Justine to Serena and back again. Clearly he didn't like the situation, but the basis for his ill humour was yet to be determined. Serena couldn't help tensing up. Last night she had believed that snobbery played no part in his character, that he was absolutely genuine in liking and wanting the person she was. She would not change her mind unless he changed it for her.

'Do call this yappy creature off, Nic, or haven't you learnt to control it yet?' Justine said a trifle waspishly, the shrill barking putting a crack in her perfect composure. It was instantly papered over as she switched on a condescending smile, beamed straight at Serena. 'Silly of me. I should have asked you, Serena, since you're the dog expert.'

'Shut up, Cleo!' Nic thundered.

It shocked the little terrier into jumping around to face him, the barking silenced, her little tail frantically wagging as though pleading to know what she'd done wrong. Nic bent and picked up the dog, tucking it protectively in the crook of one arm while using his other hand to calm it down, ruffling the silky hair behind her ears. Cleo responded by eagerly licking every reachable part of Nic's bare skin.

'Well, this is progress,' Justine remarked, trilling an amused laugh.

'I went to the front door, only to find your vacated SAAB parked at the steps,' Nic said tersely.

She shrugged. 'Oh, I thought I'd find you out here. Such a glorious morning!'

'Yes, it is. And I'm wondering why you've come, driving all the way from Sydney without first calling me to...'

'I just dropped in on the off-chance you were home, Nic,' she rolled out, putting on an expression of charming appeal. 'I'm on my way to Terrigal, joining friends for lunch at *The Galley*. You remember the Norths, Sonia and Joel. They're just back from racing their yacht at San Diego. And Liz and Teddy...'

Serena numbly listened to the celebrity status of Justine's *friends,* knowing this was Nic's social circle, too. An A-list luncheon party, without a doubt, and being described to tempt Nic into joining it, as well as spelling out that Serena wouldn't fit, if indeed Justine even saw *the dog-handler* as anyone to be counted.

Nic was frowning, looking impatient with Justine's spiel...or finding himself hooked on the horns of a dilemma. Inconvenient for him that Serena was still here, if he fancied taking up the invitation subtly being offered. Last night Nic had made her feel indispensible to him...or had she been fooling herself, believing in something that had only been generated by the heat of lust?

'So you're off to a luncheon with the people you like mixing with,' Nic drawled mockingly. 'Why drop in here?'

Serena's sluggish heartbeat instantly picked up. It didn't sound as if he cared for the company at all. Nor was he being receptive to having Justine's presence thrust upon him.

'Don't be like that, Nic,' she cajoled, pouting with sexy appeal. 'I'm sorry I left without saying goodbye after my weekend with you.'

'I took goodbye for granted from the manner of your departure,' he answered coldly.

They'd had a fight, Serena swiftly surmised. Was Nic's pride at stake here, or was he truly finished with Justine?

'I'm sorry. Okay? I lost my temper...' She raised her hands in apologetic appeal. 'Put it down to not much sleep because of the dog.' She forced a smile at Cleo. 'Now that you've got her tamed...'

'Thanks to Serena,' Nic slid in and pointedly turned his gaze to her, looking determined that she not be ignored or left out of this conversation any longer.

'Yes. I can see you're very grateful to her. Nice of you to invite her for a swim in the pool,' Justine said dismissively, her eyes glittering green daggers at Serena as she condescendingly added, 'But you're not expecting to stay all day, are you, dear? You won't mind if I carry Nic off to lunch with our friends?'

Nic came in hard and fast. 'I've invited Serena to stay *all* day and I'm not the least bit interested in joining your party, which I would have told you if you'd called instead of coming here uninvited and making unwarranted assumptions,' he stated tersely.

Justine sighed and tried a silky challenge, placing a hand on a provocatively jutting hip. 'Why wouldn't I think I'd be welcome, Nic? We have been lovers for…'

'Just give it up, Justine,' he cut in, the harsh command slightly softened by the follow-up appeal. 'Okay?'

It wasn't okay. It produced a sulky protest. 'I have apologised…'

Angry impatience burst from Nic. 'That currency won't buy you back in. I've moved on.' He flashed Serena a look that commanded her compliance with his next assertion. 'I'm very happy in Serena's company and have no wish to exchange it for anyone else's.'

Serena held her breath. Here it was—the situation punched out in no uncertain terms. Nic's handsome face looked so hard it could have been carved out of granite. Having told Justine where he was at, he wasn't about to excuse his actions, either. This declaration was a straight slap in the face to any hope or expectation of any intimacy with her being resumed. Certainly not today, anyway.

Retaliation was not slow in coming.

'Your bed feeling a bit cold, was it?' Justine mocked, her lip curling up in distaste as she subjected Serena to a contemptuous dismissal. 'And, of course, *you'd* be only too happy to oblige him. Panting for the chance, no doubt, just like a bitch on heat.'

'That's enough!' Nic rasped.

'Oh, for God's sake, Nic!' Her hands scissored total exasperation. 'You can't be serious about taking up with *her!* She might be handy for sex and useful for looking after the dog, but...'

'Serena is a great deal more than that and I am very serious about holding on to her as long as I can,' Nic cut in with such fury in his voice it startled Cleo into barking again.

'This is ridiculous!' Justine glared at the silky terrier, then carried her glare to Nic, returning his fury with all the fury of a woman scorned. 'You're turning *me* down for a common local tart who works with stinky little animals?'

'Serena happens to be the most *un*common woman I've ever met. And be warned about that *tart* crack, Justine. What goes around comes around and if I hear it repeated in public, you'll find yourself tagged with something similarly unpleasant.'

Shock had Justine gaping at him. 'You'd humiliate me...for her?'

'You start it... I'll deliver it back to you in spades. What's more, I wouldn't carry on about stinky little animals if I were you, because you're making a nasty stink yourself right now and I'm finding it extremely *ugly.*'

The *ugly* word was meant to hit hard and it did. Justine visibly recoiled from the offensiveness of it. Serena couldn't help feeling justice had been served, considering the offensiveness the other woman had dished out.

Nevertheless, a haughty recovery was quickly effected. An arrogant pride stamped itself on the beautiful face. The glorious mane of hair was tossed in disdain of everything that had been said as she shook

her head and proceeded to adopt a mock-indul-
gent tone.

'Well, I must admit I'm not enamoured with the
dog situation you have here so I'll overlook this temporary aberration of yours, Nic. Call me when you
get back to Sydney and we'll pick up from there.'

'It won't happen,' Nick told her with emphatic finality.

Justine chose to ignore him, swinging on her heel
and swanning off in catwalk mode, taking her own
path around the house again, flaunting *her* message
that Justine Knox was not about to be shown the door
and she'd still be on call when Nic came to his senses.

It wasn't only Serena watching her go. Nick's gaze
was glued to Justine's back until it disappeared from
view. Was he wondering if he'd made the right decision? Angry that he'd been caught in a hard place,
knowing he'd come off as a real slime if he'd tried
to wriggle out of or skate over what had been going
on with Serena?

An engine was loudly revved, a decisive signal that
Justine was, indeed, on her way out. Nic set Cleo
down on the patio, a somewhat premature move since
the little terrier went hurtling off around the house to
chase the car and bark it off the premises. Nic
shrugged and shook his head at the unstoppable action, then started down the steps to the pool level,
grimacing his displeasure at having been forced to
deal with such a scene.

'Don't take anything Justine said to heart, Serena.
That was all just bitchy grandstanding,' he said dismissively.

'You really are finished with her, Nic?'

He looked startled that she could think otherwise. 'No way in the world would I ever get back with Justine Knox.' He frowned at her possible uncertainty. 'You can't believe I would?'

She grimaced. 'I don't want to.'

'Then don't. You're the only woman I want.' A wicked smile broke across his face as he reached out and scooped her into his embrace. 'If you need more convincing...'

The only woman I want... music to her ears, a joyful beat through her heart. She linked her hands around his neck, suddenly yearning to hold on to him forever, though she couldn't help thinking they would be torn asunder sooner or later.

'You know Justine won't be the only one to say such things about me, Nic. You'll be answering to this kind of prejudice for as long as you have me with you. It's about who you are and who I'm not, and nothing you can say or do will really change that.'

'You're wrong, Serena.' His eyes burned with the belief in his own power to beat any criticism of their relationship. 'I promise you, any controversy about our pairing will fade very quickly.'

'You can't dominate people's minds...alter ingrained attitudes.'

He stroked her cheek, smiling with a kind of whimsical indulgence as though she were a child he was instructing. 'You see the power of wealth, Serena, but you don't understand it. Not from the inside as I do. If my family accepts you, believe me, everyone else will be only too happy to acknowledge you and treat you with enormous respect.'

She shook her head, thinking his family's acceptance a highly unlikely eventuality. 'I don't see how that could happen.'

He kissed her doubting eyes closed, kissed the end of her nose, kissed the fear from her mouth, then murmured with passionate confidence, 'Trust me. I have the perfect plan.'

CHAPTER SEVENTEEN

'Wow, little sister!' Michelle exclaimed with a huge sigh of feeling as they finally reached the luxurious bedroom suite assigned to them. 'The Morettis certainly throw everything into celebrating a family wedding. This has been totally, totally overwhelming!'

Serena laughed. Over the past few months, she had gradually become used to the Italian effusiveness in Nic's family, the hugging, the kissing, the generous gift-giving, and she had learnt to gracefully accept the unbelievable extravagance in the planning for this wedding—hers and Nic's. However, she well understood Michelle's reaction to the culmination of all these plans.

Outside, in the grounds of the Moretti compound on the Sydney Harbour shoreline, was a fabulous white marquee, festooned with flowers and thousands of fairy lights, filled with people in dazzling evening wear, the best French champagne flowing from an endless store, gourmet food being constantly offered and served, a variety of live bands providing music for dancing and singing. It was an event, the like of which neither of them had ever experienced before, let alone played star roles in it.

'Did I get through it okay?' Michelle asked a trifle anxiously.

'You were great,' Serena warmly assured her sister. 'The perfect matron of honour.'

Michelle grinned. 'Well, I'd have to say you're the most spectacular bride I've ever seen.'

Serena grinned back. 'I could see Nic's mother adored all this elaborate beading and lace. She just beamed with pleasure when I chose it.'

'It's pure fairy-tale princess stuff. And it's obvious Nic's mum adores you, too.'

'God knows why, but she seemed delighted to welcome me into the family right from the start. Nic's dad, too.'

'Well, they might be filthy rich, but they are nice people,' Michelle declared. 'Now let's get you out of your bridal gear and into your going away outfit.'

This was a frivolous little dress in shell pink silk chiffon, shoe-string shoulder straps, frills around the bodice, frills around the hem of the skirt. After the exquisite, form-fitting formality of the ceremonial bridal gown, it was a relief to simply slide into a dress that skimmed her figure and felt frothy and feminine. Relaxing.

'Don't forget you still have to throw your bouquet,' Michelle reminded her.

'I'll throw it to you,' Serena promised, hoping her older sister would marry Gavin who seemed to share many interests with her. He was here at the wedding with his daughter, who thought it was *excellent* that Erin, her best friend, was the flower girl at the ceremony.

'No need.' Michelle's eyes sparkled above suddenly pink cheeks. 'Gavin proposed to me tonight. I said yes.'

'Oh, that's marvellous!' Serena threw her arms

around her sister and hugged hard. 'I hope you'll both be very happy together.'

Michelle hugged back. 'You, too, with Nic.'

Emotion welled between them.

'Maybe we've reached our journey's end, Michelle.'

'You mean since Mum and Dad died.'

'And David.'

'Do you feel you really belong with Nic, Serena?'

'Yes, I do.'

'Gavin gives me that feeling, too. Like finally filling what's been missing in my life...coming home.'

So much had been missing that Nic had filled, Serena thought as they returned to the marquee. He made her feel protected, provided for, looked after, understood. He was like a rock of absolute and enduring stability, unshakable in bestowing his love and loyalty and support. She'd given him her trust and the reward of that act of faith was still awesome to her. Even his formidable family had welcomed her into their midst without so much as a raised eyebrow.

She smiled as she glanced over at his parents, thinking how lucky she was to have met their son. Beside them were Angelina and Ward, with Cleo on a white satin leash, Nic having insisted the dog be here since the little terrier had been a prime mover in their relationship. And was much beloved by his sister.

They all caught her smile and smiled back. There had not once been any criticism of her from any of these people, no patronising, no hint of condescension. She was sure in her own mind that Nic had made this happen for her. He'd spoken of the power of wealth, and its buying power was all around her, but in her heart, she couldn't believe he could *buy* her this level of genuine approval.

Having completed the last bridal act of throwing her bouquet, she headed straight for him and he left the group of guests he'd been chatting to, moving to meet her, his dark eyes locking onto hers, and what she felt coming from him was the power of love, not wealth.

'One more dance with you in that flirty little dress before we go,' he said with a sexy suggestiveness that had her whole body humming with desire for him as he swept her into his arms and twirled her onto the dance-floor.

He was a superb dancer, fantastic at everything, Serena thought giddily. 'Thank you for loving me, Nic,' she said in a rush of sheer happiness. 'And for bringing me into your wonderful family and making me feel I belong with you.'

'You do belong with me.' He grinned, his whole face lit with triumphant pleasure. 'We're married.'

She laughed at his delight in this achievement. 'So we are. And I love my husband very much.'

'Rightly so. It wouldn't be fair if you didn't since I've applied myself so diligently to winning your love.'

'Now why would you do that when I presented so many problems?' she teased, adoring him for wanting the role of her knight in shining armour.

He heaved a mock sigh. 'I'm a sucker for challenges.'

She arched her eyebrow. 'Don't you think tying yourself to me for life is taking a challenge too far?'

'I'm into bondage with you. Can't help myself. My soul says you're my soul mate, now and forever. If marriage is a challenge, I'm definitely up for it as long as you're my wife.'

He rolled out the words with such relish Serena had to laugh again, but her soul was deeply stirred by his commitment to her and silently echoed it—now and forever. Nic clasped her closer and whirled her around in a burst of exhilaration that left them both simmering with the desire to be by themselves and make wild passionate love together.

'Just tell me one more thing before we take our leave of everyone,' Serena begged.

'I'll grant you one minor delay.'

'Your family seems to think I'm the best thing that's ever happened to you. And I don't know why.'

'That's easy.' His eyes twinkled with devilish delight. 'I had the perfect plan to win their instant approval of our marriage, and to regard you as manna from heaven.'

'Manna from heaven?'

'Serena, the Morettis are of strong Italian blood and the big thing in their lives is family.'

'But I don't have much in the way of family. Only Michelle and…'

'The point is, my darling wife, you're keen to provide one.'

She looked her bewilderment. 'I don't understand.'

'It's a great sorrow to my parents that Angelina and Ward can't have children. So what did I tell them? Apart from the fact that I loved you and couldn't imagine a life without you at my side… I told them what you wanted most was to be the mother of my children and have a houseful of kids.'

'Children,' she repeatedly dazedly. 'Oh, my God! What if I can't have them?'

'Trust me,' Nic said with supreme confidence. 'I'm very potent.'

Trust…that was what it had been about all along…and it worked.

Serena smiled at her all powerful husband. 'You're right, Nic,' she agreed with the same supreme confidence he had shown. 'You *are* very potent.'

Sydney Morning Herald
Personal Columns
Births

Moretti—On the first day of January to very proud parents, Serena and Nic—triplets—a fine son, Lucas Angelo, and two beautiful daughters, Isabella Rose and Katriona Louise—three wonderful grandchildren for Frank and Lucia.

Modern Romance™
...seduction and
passion guaranteed

Tender Romance™
...love affairs that
last a lifetime

Medical Romance™
...medical drama
on the pulse

Historical Romance™
...rich, vivid and
passionate

Sensual Romance™
...sassy, sexy and
seductive

Blaze Romance™
...the temperature's
rising

27 new titles every month.

Live the emotion

MILLS & BOON®

MB3

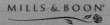

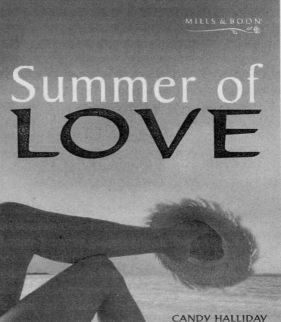

MILLS & BOON

Summer of
LOVE

CANDY HALLIDAY

HOLLY JACOBS

CATHIE LINZ

ELISE TITLE

Available from 16th May 2003

*Available at most branches of WH Smith,
Tesco, Martins, Borders, Eason, Sainsbury's
and all good paperback bookshops.*

FREE!

2 Books
and a surprise gift!

We would like to take this opportunity to thank you for reading this Mills & Boon® book by offering you the chance to take TWO more specially selected titles from the Modern Romance™ series absolutely FREE! We're also making this offer to introduce you to the benefits of the Reader Service™—

- ★ FREE home delivery
- ★ FREE gifts and competitions
- ★ FREE monthly Newsletter
- ★ Books available before they're in the shops
- ★ Exclusive Reader Service discount

Accepting these FREE books and gift places you under no obligation to buy; you may cancel at any time, even after receiving your free shipment. Simply complete your details below and return the entire page to the address below. *You don't even need a stamp!*

YES! Please send me 2 free Modern Romance books and a surprise gift. I understand that unless you hear from me, I will receive 4 superb new titles every month for just £2.60 each, postage and packing free. I am under no obligation to purchase any books and may cancel my subscription at any time. The free books and gift will be mine to keep in any case.

P3ZEB

Ms/Mrs/Miss/Mr ....Initials................................

BLOCK CAPITALS PLEASE

Surname..

Address...

....

....Postcode ....

Send this whole page to:
UK: The Reader Service, FREEPOST CN81, Croydon, CR9 3WZ
EIRE: The Reader Service, PO Box 4546, Kilcock, County Kildare (stamp required)

Offer not valid to current Reader Service subscribers to this series. We reserve the right to refuse an application and applicants must be aged 18 years or over. Only one application per household. Terms and prices subject to change without notice. Offer expires 29th August 2003. As a result of this application, you may receive offers from Harlequin Mills & Boon and other carefully selected companies. If you would prefer not to share in this opportunity please write to The Data Manager at the address above.

Mills & Boon® is a registered trademark owned by Harlequin Mills & Boon Limited.
Modern Romance ™ is being used as a trademark.